THE
LAST WOMAN
WARRIOR
OF THE
LIBURNIANS

THE
LAST WOMAN
WARRIOR
OF THE
LIBURNIANS

ANDREJA AUSTIN

Published by:
Andreja Austin

Santa Fe, NM

For information about this title, contact the publisher:
vaandreja7@gmail.com

Cover and interior design by The Book Cover Whisperer:
OpenBookDesign.biz

The Last Woman Warrior of the Liburnians

Library of Congress Control Number: 2024906752

979-8-218-97177-9 Paperback

Printed in the United States of America

Published by:
Andreja Austin

FIRST EDITION, 2024

To my parents, I am grateful for the love and inspiration they gave to me during their lifetime

CONTENTS

It is said, "Amazon women are legendary;
Liburnians are history..."

THE WOMAN WARRIOR
WE HAVEN'T SEEN
BEFORE

When you start reading the novel, *The Last Woman Warrior of the Liburnians*, you will first get an impression that you have found a genuine woman's fiction novel, giving a realistic view of a modern-day life. Just a few pages after, you realize you were wrong and have an unusual love, fiction novel in your hands. In the next chapter, you will find out that this was not true either, for this is a thriller with supernatural elements, or maybe an adventure novel in feminine Elmore Leonard style.

And then, reading further, you would realize that all your impressions were right – and wrong, as well. The truth is that the novel, *The Last Woman Warrior of the Liburnians*, takes you halfway around the world, from Ugljan to Jerusalem and New York; the truth is that it guides you through a story searching for a young man who mysteriously disappeared; the truth is that it reveals a love story beyond time and space. All of that is true. But the truth is also that all of that is not the main focus of the novel: this is only incidental. In other words, its main female character discovers, through her surprising adventures, her origin, the heritage of the ancient Liburnians and their deities that guide and protect her and accepts her role as – the last woman warrior of the Liburnians.

We don't know much about the Liburnians and their mythology. The knowledge that we have doesn't always come from reliable sources. However, the author of this novel used the knowledge that was available and added the elements of spirituality of different cultures, thus creating a combination, typical for today, in which spiritual literature fans would undoubtedly each find something for themselves. On the trail of Paulo Coelho, or maybe even James Redfield, and at the same time with a very distinctive point of view and characteristically feminine approach to the story, the novel of Andreja Austin fills a much-needed gap in Croatian popular literature. This gives our readers the opportunity to experience something they haven't had the chance to see from the pen of a Croatian, female writer.

Milena Benini

PROLOGUE

News of the upcoming full Moon eclipse was broadcast on the nightly TV news. It was March 2006. Looking at the pictures on the television screen, you could gain a clear idea of this extraordinary and impressive event. It probably would not have gotten my attention if I hadn't noticed how astonishing the whole scene was when it appeared on the TV screen: a luminous disc floating upon the vault of heaven, changing colors from gray moondust to scarlet sunset. "The faster the Earth's shadow blocks the Moon, the more intense will be the transformation. It will reflect strongly on the lives of everybody and on the whole planet," the voice from the screen stated.

It crossed my mind how surprising it was to hear them talk about it in such an unusual way on the news. It was certainly not an everyday event; maybe it was even an omen. I approached the window. A weird sensation of fear passed through me. I tried not to give in to it and to continue, enjoying the beautiful spring scenery – the first stars in the late evening. The voice from the screen continued, "It wouldn't be so unusual if it weren't for the occurrence of a double astronomical event. The planet Pluto, the symbol of destruction, will square the Moon and will come into opposition with the Sun.

"Astrologically speaking, the full Moon can block our consciousness, bringing hidden tensions to the surface. On the world scene, clashes between the great powers may occur. After the time of destruction, there will be a time of revival. The battle of Armageddon begins."

I was still standing at the window, watching the glittering sky hang over the island[1]. I was alone in my grandmother's house, where I had been coming since my early youth when I needed a refuge for contemplation.

The night was "letting its hair down." The dazzling display of stars was bringing back memories. I felt an amazing feeling awaken in me. I wasn't sure whether it was caused by the ecstatic moonlight atmosphere or by a heavenly source. A peace came over me. The blessed silence filled the air. I recalled him – not knowing why exactly at this time. I recalled Pandit[2] Sati

---

[1] The Ugljan Island is part of the archipelago of Zadar, Croatia. It is located in the heart of the Adriatic Sea. In this brochure the reader can learn more about the region: https://www.zadar.hr/.

[2] Pandit, Skt. – a wise, learned Brahmin in India.

and his veiled dresses that were permeated with the fragrance of sandalwood.

My thoughts reverted to the past days when I was in my final year of specialization in psychiatry. I was studying Eastern spiritual techniques, seeking to reveal the secrets of the psyche. I met Pandit Sati by chance after an unplanned visit to the theater on one gloomy early Sunday evening. He was a guest performer. I wasn't sure whether it was after Dostoevsky's play *Demons*[3] or Bresan's[4] play *Devil* at the Zagreb Youth Theater[5]. I went to his performance out of simple curiosity. He gave me a mantra, something very much like a prayer to be spoken aloud.

These images from the past disappeared. It seemed as if recalling the mantra brought me back from the depth of the Self. Some invisible hand touched my brow. I felt instant peace when I heard something like God's voice, "There will be an eclipse. An opportunity for Self-realization will be revealed to you. You will

---

[3] A novel by the famous Russian novelist, short story writer, essayist and philosopher Fyodor Dostoevsky (1821-1881), first published in Russian in 1872 as *Besy*.

[4] Ivo Bresan (1936-2017) - a play *The Devil at the Faculty of Philosophy* by Ivo Bresan, a Croatian playwright, novelist, and screenwriter.

[5] The Zagreb Youth Theater, popularly called ZeKaeM Theater, is a modern theater situated in the very center of the city of Zagreb, the capital of Croatia.

have a clear sense of your purpose. It will give you strength and power to face the challenges on your path to realization."

The voice was reverberating throughout space accompanied by the loud chanting of the mantra, as if by its echo it would embrace the Moon that blocked its way. Bells in nearby bell towers were ringing, calling people to the late service. The echo of the bells spread, filling the space, and then, disappeared over the top of the country roofs. With it faded away a vague memory of an image of a dark-skinned man who was radiating love and fulfillment.

A
SORCERESS
FROM
UGLJAN

———

I

THE BOOK OF GRANDMOTHER LUCIJA

It was an omen – seeing Venus at dawn, with the wind caressing my sleepy eyes as they looked for the smile of the first ray of the Sun. I woke up early, as though I knew I could catch, at the last moment, a glimmer of Venus light vanishing in the dazzling light of the rising Sun.

A sacred silence pervaded the space, followed by the quiet gallop of the sea breeze. The wind was blowing, casting up the bluish-white foam, carrying the song from the depths of the sea.

I used to wake up in the early spring mornings and take a bike ride to the footsteps of Kuran Hill[6]. There were stones scattered along the hill; it was said they were the burial mounds of the ancient Liburnians[7]. I so

---

[6] The prehistoric ruins on the hill of Kuran.

[7] The Liburnians were the ancient inhabitants of the region

enjoyed this countryside. I went here whenever I came
to Preko from Zadar[8]. But, in recent visits I noticed
that the environment had changed. Behind the burial
mound where an imposing, lonesome cedar tree was
standing, a vast forest unraveled its crowns. Old-age
pine trees were rising into the skies, sweeping up into
the first clouds, as if they would stop time to let me
pass through their territory. I could smell the gentle
scent of pine all along the way... The Sun, seeming
shy, was barely glimpsed through the thick branches.
It disappeared just behind St. Mihovil. The sky suddenly darkened and I hurried to get home before an
approaching storm.

Tired after my long ride, I refreshed myself and
changed clothes in the bathroom. A cold apple ginger
tea after the bath invigorated me and worked up my
appetite. My favorite cucumber salad with seaweed
brought back my energy and I cheered up.

I was looking forward to going for another bike
ride in the afternoon. It was just a matter of time

---

between the Istria (the peninsula in the Adriatic Sea) and
the river Titus (the Krka river) in what is now Croatia. Much
of their history has been lost; the region along the northern
Adriatic coast in Europe, in modern Croatia, is circled on the
map: "image: Freepik.com". This part of Croatia is to the right
of the Italian booth.

[8] The town of Preko on the Ugljan Island is located opposite
Zadar.

before it would start raining, for which I would need
a good warm coat. Not knowing where to find such a
thing, I remembered my grandmother's cellar. It was a
secret underground room, where grandmother Lucija
kept all kinds of things. It hadn't been touched since
my grandfather died, five years ago.

I went slowly down the stairs to the cellar. I could
feel the penetrating, damp cold in the hall, like a ghost

from the past. I cleared away a shabby pile of stored things. I moved a ceiling beam out of the way. It had fallen long ago, rotted by dampness. That was when my attention rested on an old chest. It lay in the corner, hidden from curious eyes, wrapped in a dusty, red cloth. Maybe here I would find a cloak.

I blew away the thick layer of dust and carefully opened the chest. There was a book inside, covered by a book jacket of lace which was interwoven like a magic cobweb around the white pages. It looked untouched, not showing any signs of age. Even more strange were its pages. They were filled with symbols, graphic signs, similar to Braille letters. Turning the thin pages, I had a vision of my grandmother's mysterious figure, her face radiating celestial wisdom. I remembered the rumors that were going around the village about her miraculous powers and the blissful energy she exuded.

Leafing through the book, I found her photo – a beautiful, young woman much as I remembered her. Standing under an olive tree, she was tall, with deep almond eyes, and an expressive chin which I inherited from her. Her long, thick hair was bound in a linen scarf embellished with white lace and she wore traditional black attire with white trim and a wide, woolen belt over a simple bell-sleeved linen shirt.

The book had embossed initials on the first page with the two letters "L" outlined in golden threads, with one letter reversed. The letters had the shape of a snake-like tail. Instead of an inscription, there were words from Revelation: "Do not seal up the words of prophecy in this book, because the time is near."[9] It was obviously something mysterious. I read until it became dark. Then, I took the book and went to the deck, where I spent the rest of the night in the open loggia with its overhanging roof.

The sound of the waves lulled me to sleep. They were driven by a strong wind blowing off the shore which changed to a stiff breeze. The wind was blowing in gusts. It sounded like a sea organ playing.

I looked toward the slightly opened window which was squeaking to the beat of the wind. The squeaking was accompanied by the rustling of the curtains. Through the transparent, gossamer threads of the curtains I could see the beautiful view of Zadar, cloaked in the light of the stars.

The town rose above the rough sea, proudly showing its towers. There was an atmosphere, of a timeless void which filled the air with the silent whisper of the wind. Wrapped up in a veil woven by memories, I immersed myself in the magical serenity,

[9] https://biblehub.com/revelation/22-10.htm.

re-experiencing the smells of my childhood, the scent of rosemary, dew from the sea, lavender and olives. In my dreamlike state I could hear the rattling of my grandmother's pots in the kitchen as she stirred with her wooden ladle. Grandmother Lucija was making a miraculous potion while looking at me from the corner of her elusive eye. Her gaze was on my heavy eyelids, sending me thoughts from a distance. Half-asleep, I could hear her talking about how I was chosen by Divine Providence for a big mission. I should go forward in her image with trust and help her in the battle to save people's souls on Earth. Then she left. Her hair, carried by the breath of eternity, was fluttering behind her as her illuminated figure slowly disappeared from my sight.

IN THE FOOTSTEPS OF THE LIBURNIANS

The day started with my hurried preparation for the scientific conference on ethno-medicine that was about to begin at the Faculty of Philosophy[10]. When I came home, I changed into a light blue Chanel suit which I carefully kept for such occasions. I pulled my hair up into a high bun and put on light blue sunglasses in a shade that matched the dress. I grabbed the keys to my Smart car and headed towards the Faculty building.

I arrived at the very moment when the Head of the Department of Ethnology, Dr. Matija Sandalic, was introduced and greeted with loud applause. I pushed through to the center of the hall, smiling at those who let me through to my seat. As soon as I

---

[10] The Faculty of Philosophy in Zadar, one of the oldest in Europe was founded in 1396 by the Dominican order.

sat down, a young man with a beautiful profile got up from the seat next to me. He looked very elegant in a Russian shirt with a white collar which accentuated his well-built figure. When he passed by, he looked at me with penetrating black eyes. I noticed one slightly crossed eye, an unpleasant handicap without which he would have embodied perfection. He seemed somehow familiar, but I couldn't remember where I had seen him. I finally recognized him when he was called up on stage. It was Mihovil Dorcic, the junior researcher of the Faculty of Philosophy in Zagreb[11]. His area of special interest was medical anthropology. It was announced that he was about to give a lecture on magical, cultural paradigms in the treatment of disease in archaic cultures in southeastern Europe.

Attracted to the young man's appearance, I was watching him closely, more than I was listening to him. However, my attention became focused during the last part of the lecture on the ancient Liburnians. There is not much written evidence of their history, although they reached a high cultural level in prehistoric times. They flourished as a maritime nation

---

[11] The Faculty of Philosophy or the Faculty of Humanities and Social Sciences in Zagreb was established in 1874. It is one of the faculties of the University of Zagreb, one of the oldest universities in Europe, founded in the second half of the 17th century.

from the ninth to the fifth century B.C., when they dominated the Adriatic Sea. At the time of Christ they came under the rule of the Romans. The first records of their medicine date back to this time. As with most of the nations of this region, it is presumed that their medicine was based on magical-religious beliefs. The beliefs were most likely centered upon ancestor worship. What is especially interesting is that the cult was maintained by women. They honored women Goddesses, among whom were Anzotika the Roman Venus or Greek Aphrodite, Ika or Diana, Irija and Sentona. It is quite likely that the women assumed the role of sorceress. Like ancient shamans in ecstatic cults, their souls would leave their bodies and go in search of the souls of the ill.

The Liburnians developed their own medical concepts to explain disease. The major symptom of the disease was thought to be the loss of one's soul due to spell or obsession. This concept has been strongly held in national beliefs.

The rest of the conference offered several interesting lectures. Mihovil's lecture, however, surpassed all the others. I couldn't help feeling that it was in part pseudoscientific and quite scientific. I hoped we would have a chance to talk about everything soon. The opportunity presented itself at a banquet.

❀ ❀ ❀

I ARRIVED AT THE five-star, President Hotel a little earlier than the other guests. The banquet was held in its restaurant, Vivaldi. The place could not have been more beautiful surrounded by a forest of pines and with stunning views of islands in a tranquil bay.

Suddenly footsteps were heard through the deafening silence, followed by the agitating waves in the distance.

"Inraptured from the beauty of the scene?" the voice behind me said.

I turned around and saw Mihovil approaching, hurrying along the gravel path leading to the hotel. He had a pleasant, refined bearing. His voice was pensive as if he would like to share with me the miraculous moment.

"Good evening, young man," I stepped nearer to him and offered him a hand. He greeted me with a gentle handshake that spoke louder than words. In his discreet, yet evocative gaze, I met the hidden desire of exquisite passion. He looked at me and saw the expression on my face. I forgot myself for a moment and said warmly in return, "It's time. Let's go."

We went to the private dining-room where our colleagues awaited us. In the intimate atmosphere of the restaurant, I relaxed and opened up to Mihovil. It seemed as though he already knew something about me. He was curious about my trips into the unconscious and my meditation experiences, which he may have read about in my publications.

Mihovil's professional interest appeared to me as the habitual interest of a junior researcher. I was more surprised by his undisguised interest in me as a woman. He was silently gazing at me with his piercing black eyes, beaming some secret, unfathomable power. His alluring smile was like the flickering flame of a candle; his naturally pink lips were soft as satin. He exuded a romantic ecstasy and sentimentality with an impulsiveness and delight. Completely enchanted with his appearance, I felt more feminine in his presence. I felt like the sensual woman in the English painting facing us on the wall.

"May I ask you to dance?" Mihovil turned to me and gently touched my wrist.

"Yes, of course," I answered excitedly, heading with him towards the ballroom where Vivaldi's *Four Seasons*[12] could be heard.

Music by Strauss[13] soon began playing. I clung

---

[12] *The Four Seasons* by the Italian baroque composer Antonio Vivaldi (1678-1741) is a group of four violin concerti composed in 1723.

[13] Johann Strauss II or Johann Strauss Jr. (1825-1899), the son

to Mihovil and surrendered to the waltz melody, as a flood of pleasant sensations began filling my whole body. Nevertheless, in the young man's arms, I felt not myself.

Mihovil continued, as if he sensed my thoughts, "I know how you feel. We are similar, if not the same."

"What do you mean?"

"We are related; you felt it instinctively."

Mihovil looked at me, and I had a sensation of an increasing flow of energy up my spinal cord. I stared into his deep black eyes that were looking at me like two black opals of variable colors of a spectrum. Dazzled by their brilliance, I fell into a hypnotic sleep. His eyes were upon me, inviting me with unfathomable longing. A cool sensation washed over me, filling me with passion. The gentle touch of his fingers as he gazed into my eyes aroused me.

I continued, "How do you know?"

"I can feel your strength and purity. Forgive my indiscretion, but I can tell you that your kundalini energy[14] is so pure that you are almost like a Divine being. I feel a connection with you."

---

of Johann Strauss I (1804-1849), was a famous composer of the Viennese waltzes and operettas. His famous waltz, "The Blue Danube" was composed in 1866.

[14] Kundalini, Skt. – "coiled up", "coiling like a snake" – life energy.

"Who are you, and who are we?"

"I don't know. Maybe you can help me. Something tells me that we are the offspring of a small nation. We come from this island, and we are related. The fact of the matter is that we are a rather small group of people scattered throughout the world who have to find each other."

Mihovil embraced me more firmly and continued in his deep baritone, "Antonija, I am in Zadar for one more day. Can we meet?"

We left the hall hugging and went along a sea path.

"Yes, tomorrow," I said, taking a long breath, but I couldn't finish my thought. I could feel a kiss followed by a gentle touch on my shoulders. Just this one touch was enough to explode my feelings and cause the flaring up of a discovery of an exceedingly beautiful blessing of love. I felt Mihovil's muffled passion. His kisses had a mild taste of salt. He seemed like an asexual, supernatural being.

"See you tomorrow!" I could read his lips. He then waved good-bye, walking away along the path that led to a rock cliff.

THE SUN WAS WELL above the horizon when I lazily stretched out in the soft bed. I thought I would sleep a little longer. I turned to my other side when the telephone rang. Clumsily, as I was wrapped up in sheets, I grabbed the phone. The familiar voice of my friend Alka blared from the phone's speaker.

"Antonija, where are you? What happened? We all were waiting for you at the morning lecture. Since you didn't come, the first report was submitted by the Head of the Ethnology Department, Professor Matija Sandalic. As soon as he finished, we rushed off to find Mihovil, thinking that you were together. But we couldn't find him either. He disappeared without a trace. Antonija, you surprised us yesterday. You two were very beautiful together, like two doves in love. I am happy for you."

"Alka, I cannot talk now. I'll call you."

I was still for a moment, exhaling into the silent phone. Alka was thoughtful and gave me a little more time to come around. I was staring at my reflection in the mirror on the opposite side of the room. I ran my hand through my long, wavy hair that fell around my shoulders. I pulled the sheet off of my bare breast. I felt excitement, recalling the memory of that touch, a cold touch and the kisses with the scent of the sea salt. With physical excitement, I felt a silent flicker in my heart, an uncontrollable desire for a pure, etheric love I had never felt before. Yet it was followed by a strange feeling of anxiety that I couldn't explain. Moreover, I didn't know how to explain it to any of my dear friends, so I decided it would be better not to reveal anything related to Mihovil.

The ring of my cellphone interrupted my thoughts. That was Mihovil's message that he would arrive in a few minutes. I had enough time to put on makeup and a silk cloak. I went to the door. I looked through the window of the glass door which I always used out of precaution. There was Mihovil with a bunch of beautiful blue roses.

"For you, Antonija. I especially chose them in your favorite color," he kissed me and handed me the flowers.

"Thank you, Mihovil," I greeted him with a kiss. "Have a seat."

"Dear Antonija, isn't it time to be on a first-name basis?" he turned to me and seated himself in the velvet-like chair where I liked to read.

"Of course, Mihovil," I replied with a smile, holding the roses. Approaching the bookshelf, I wanted to reach for a vase when I accidentally knocked a book off the little serving table. I had left it there, wrapped in the red grandmother's cloth after I had come back from the island.

Mihovil jumped up and reached for the book. He

picked it up in his arms as though he were hugging a woman around her waist. Then he silently put it on his lap. He unwrapped the cloth and began turning the pages. A flame of exalted happiness brought a smile to his face; he said to me, "Antonija, where did you find this book?"

"In Preko, in the cellar of grandmother Lucija's house," I explained.

"Grandmother Lucija?" Mihovil paused. He pulled himself up, giving me a look of a wise teacher who keeps a vigilant, protective eye on us. He continued in a steady tone, with a gentle, enthusiastic voice, "Well, Antonija, your grandmother was a sorceress, a woman keeper of an archaic tradition of mantra chanting which was passed on in these islands from generation to generation from a female line. I know this from my grandmother Ivka's storytelling. She was the last sorceress from Ugljan. After her death, the tradition became extinct."

"A sorceress?"

"Yes, a sorceress. She knew spells and sorcery and was able to heal people of many diseases. She was also successful in the treatment of psychosomatic diseases which I have been writing about recently."

"In the article that you presented at the conference that stirred up such strong feelings?"

"The book will stir them up even more if we successfully decipher it."

"But inside the book are only the symbols. They resemble the Braille system[15] for the blind."

"Antonija, at first sight it seems as if it is an archaic dialect of a primordial language. It is not known who the first speakers were. These islands in Croatia were inhabited by the ancient Liburnians. It's possible that it was preserved in their linguistic tradition. Maybe we are its last speakers."

"We?"

"In fact, you. I have to correct myself."

"Me?"

"Yes, you. The book didn't come by chance into your hands."

"Exactly, but it's not proof of my language skills."

"Unless it manifests itself in mantras."

"In mantras? I don't know any mantras. In fact..."

"What's the matter?"

"Nothing..." I paused, remembering the mantras. An idea struck me, as the image of Pandit Sati in front of me took on a more definite shape. "Something like meditation mantra chanting?"

---

[15] The Braille system for the blind is a system of raised-dot writing devised by Louis Braille (1809-1852). The system was first published in 1829.

"Yes, like meditation mantra chanting in the Indian tradition through which you harmonize yourself with the Divine vibrations. You already know it. You just have to rekindle the ancestors' traditions inside you."

Mihovil's thoughts were wandering. He continued in excitement, "It's not a coincidence that we are speaking of this today. I almost forgot. Isn't today an Eclipse?"

"Yes, the Red Eclipse. It is said to be the mark of the Armageddon."

"Armageddon?"

"Yes, the famous battle mentioned in Revelation[16] which is symbolically a harbinger of the end of time."

Mihovil's cellphone rang. He reluctantly put his hand in the pocket. He answered after the third ring. I heard a man's raised voice at the other end of the line.

"It's time, Mihovil. I am waiting for you downstairs."

"Do you have to go?"

"I have stayed too long already. I have to go to Zagreb. We'll continue next weekend. I'll call you."

"Take care!"

"Don't worry!" Mihovil greeted me, throwing a kiss from the threshold.

---

[16] https://biblehub.com/revelation/16-16.htm.

INITIATION

It was almost morning when I awoke with a start, wearily rubbing my eyes. The rays of morning light were sneaking through the shutters. They spread out into a spectrum of colors, from dark-red to yellowish moonlight, illuminating the room. The dense rays of light reached me, softly touching my face. It seemed as if they would permeate me completely.

The light was breaking through more and more, coming strongly, and a heaviness could be felt in the air. I surrendered unwillingly to the rays of dazzling light. They overwhelmed me as if they would take my soul completely.

I took a deep breath, trying to get up, but I didn't have enough strength. I was bewildered, thinking of a dream that I had just had. I envisioned a scary image of Lord Shiva with his two menacing eyes that were still looking at me. He had golden skin and was wearing a garland of snakelike deities from his waist to his neck. A small tongue of flame was glimmering between his eyes, hissing like a snake. He had a brilliant bracelet on each of his four arms, one around his wrist and another on his upper arm. He had a greenish goblet filled with nectar of the Gods in his hands. He was sitting in a lotus pose. He wore a giant string of beads around his waist that reached to his feet, covered with blood. He was mumbling to himself, pointing his finger at his mouth and repeating *Naga Shakti*[17].

I stood up and hurried to the prayer table in a trance-like state and reached for my brown string of beads with gold trim and reddish tassel for the prayer to the glory of Lord Shiva[18].

No sooner had I uttered a syllable, when a hymn reverberated. A wind arose and covered me with ash that seemed to be falling down from space itself. Absolute whiteness was everywhere. My consciousness expanded, and I got the feeling that with the strong sound in the right ear there was snakelike energy rising up from inside my spinal cord. A ray of light of a thousand colors shone, rising with the energy all the way up to my crown. For a moment I thought I would merge with the Universe and disappear in its wasteland, when I suddenly regained consciousness.

---

[17] Shakti, Skt. – power; primordial, creative energy.

[18] Shiva – the Supreme God in Hindu mythology, the creator and destroyer, and along with Brahma and Vishnu, considered a part of the Trinity.

I couldn't believe my eyes. I didn't know if it had been a dream or it had been real, but there was Pandit Sati standing in front of me with his hand on the top of my head. His silky floor-length dress was swinging like a wedding gown. He had a red-trimmed priestly ribbon around his neck, laced with multicolored woolen threads. His two warm brown eyes were penetrating mine, looking deep inside me. He came closer, smelling of sandalwood. The smell evoked memories of the past which I allowed to fade away and I was happy that he was right here next to me.

Pandit was speaking slowly, articulating his words carefully. I surrendered to his melodious, magically powerful voice. It sounded as though he were rhythmically repeating certain sound combinations that roused in me visions of future occurrences. I was listening to him, disbelieving my ears. I was accepting his words at an unconscious level, drifting off more and more into sleep.

"I came to you as a herald to prepare you for upcoming events. I used to come to you in dreams and thoughts and also in reality. It was a long time ago that I initiated you into meditation. You were not ready. But now you are more mature and you can understand that we are deeply connected and, that in fact, we have shared many lives together. It's time for you to accept my words. With these words you will awaken the knowledge hidden deeply inside yourself. You are consecrated to the secrets of Naga Spirits, mythological Gods. These are subtle beings of considerably higher vibrational energy than the energy of the human being. The easiest way for you would be to accept them as ancestral spirits. They will protect you and guide you on your path.

"In the esoteric sense, Naga[19] means the Serpent of Wisdom or the Initiate at the final stage of initiation. Therefore, you will have visions of snakes throughout your incarnation. You have released the power of Naga energy – the earth energy, the energy of the Serpentine Gods who control the psychic energetic barrier around the Earth's atmospheric envelope. The Earth's energy carries memories from Earth's ancient history. It can be felt as a vibration, or rhythmic echoing which can be felt only by initiates. When the time is right you can recognize it and receive it as a mantra which will give you the ability to heal."

―――――――――

[19] Naga – Serpentine Wisdom Beings are considered here in the context of the Hindu and Buddhist traditions as mythological serpentine beings which live in different places. In the occult tradition they originally signify wisdom and immortality.

I MOVED SLOWLY, LOOKING down at my hands with the string of prayer beads. I felt relief. I somehow knew that I had always been receiving this energy, but I didn't know why I forgot it.

The air still seemed to be full of Pandit's presence, like air that is electrified in the presence of an invisible entity, like a gentle flow of air, or like an aroma that permeates. My mind was wandering in search of any sign of the past etched on my memory. I glanced at the serving table. There was a book lying on the table, open to the same page where I left it the day before. I came closer. I lightly touched its dust cover and started turning the pages. Somewhere in the middle of the book, a lotus petal, casually wrapped in a pure silver cloth, fell out. A smile illuminated my face and the notion of being important to someone like your parents who always thinks about you, even if you forget about them, made my heart race.

It was Pandit Sati. Whether he came in my dream or in reality wasn't important anymore. What was important was that he had become a part of me. He made me aware of that part of me that was unknown to me before. Suddenly, I became aware of my past life where I was consecrated to the secrets of Naga Spirits. It was some kind of initiation into the Shivaist cult, after which I had had mixed feelings of bliss and restlessness.

I came closer to the serving table. I grabbed the lotus stem. In the manner of kaleidoscopic views that pass in quick succession, the pictures started changing. I was caught by a graceful feeling of joy, followed by the feeling of exalted love, like a love passion through which you fully surrender to God. I recalled the image of a man with brownish eyes, dark-colored like the dark Moon shadow. I caught my breath just thinking of him, of his arms entwined in mine in a meditative trance, twisting like a snake over my head. The image became quite clear and I saw Pandit Sati who was uttering ritual words. He gave me his hand as if he would come closer. No sooner did I feel his closeness than my heart started racing, the image disappeared, and I realized that I was alone.

I was awed by the magnificence of the idea revealed. The truth of the matter is that my consecration had been a sacrifice for the benefit of humanity. It seemed to be happening again by a twist of fate. I was aware I would have to bear a burden, but I wasn't sure if I was ready. I was overtaken by events and my intuition was telling me that now was the time.

Absorbed in thought, I didn't notice that the day had already passed. The city was turning off its lights, surrendering to the lethargy of the night. Only the voice from the TV screen was heard, reporting about the increasing wind gusts that were rising above the city walls.

MYSTICAL MANUSCRIPT

T he days were passing by in anticipation of the weekend and a call from Mihovil. The end of the month was near. After I gave up any hope, he called unexpectedly late Friday night. He apologized and announced he would come to Zadar tomorrow. He told me to bring the book with me and to come at exactly midday to the old Scientific Library[20] located at the Municipal Loggia[21].

Mihovil's call was a surprise. I was even more surprised when I came across Dr. Matija Sandalic in the library hall. He was standing on the left side of the glass door restlessly tapping his foot. He approached me and kindly shook my hand.

"Antonija, Mihovil will be here any minute. Let's go."

---

[20] The Library was founded in 1855 by Pietro Alessandro Paravia (1797-1857), a university professor in Turin.

[21] The City Loggia on the opposite side of the clock tower of the 16th century City Guard is located on the People's Square (Croatian: Narodni trg) in Zadar.

We went to the lecture hall. I was following Dr. Sandalic while looking from time to time over my shoulder. When close to the hall, I could hear quick footsteps approaching.

"Antonija, Dr. Sandalic," Mihovil's voice suddenly broke the awkward silence.

"Finally," I ran toward Mihovil and wrapped my arm firmly around his waist.

Our sweet sound kiss was followed by a pensive gaze of Doctor Sandalic. He coughed lightly and turned excitedly to me.

"Do you have it?"

"Yes, I do," I said in return, taking the book out of the red cloth. It had the same color as the lecture hall chairs that were left here after yesterday's Annual Assembly of the Zadar County Library Association.

"Antonija," Dr. Sandalic continued, "Mihovil told me about your book. Its discovery is of vital importance for the history of these former Liburnian regions. I believe that the book will shed light on some details about the origins of the Liburnians and their Croatian ethnocultural heritage. I suggest we work on the book in the library. It would be best to store it here."

"Yes, of course."

"Because of the sensitivity of work," Mihovil said, "we could meet here. I'll join whenever I can."

"Let's go," added Dr. Sandalic and took us to a small room where a table and three chairs were arranged. He laid the book on a tall stand similar to a music stand.

Silence prevailed around the table for a while. The faces of the participants resembled a bronze statue that was standing mute in the corner of the room waiting for restoration work. As Dr. Sandalic was about to speak, the door handle made a sound.

"Gentlemen, here is coffee," the librarian Milica greeted us with a smile and then she quickly exited the room.

"Well," Mihovil continued, "may we begin?"

"There is only one little problem," Dr. Sandalic answered, giving me a questionable look. "Do we have the services of a cryptographer?"

"Well, this might be a problem," Mihovil added. "We need a trustworthy person. The manuscript could draw public attention and I recommend that we not go public with the analysis results for now."

"I don't think there should be any problem. I'll call my girlfriend, Alka, a computational linguistic specialist. She will do it professionally."

"Will you call her?" Mihovil asked.

"I cannot today, but she could join us tomorrow. I will have to explain this to her. From the quick look

I had at my grandmother's book, it seemed to be a mystical, symbolically written manuscript."

"The text should be deciphered to determine the age and the writing system of the manuscript," Dr. Sandalic added. He paused; then he continued, "Antonija, I hope you will be able to work with your girlfriend and help her if necessary."

"Yes, of course," I said.

"Nice; it's a done deal. Let's go ahead with it," said Dr. Sandalic. He asked the librarian Milica to lock the room. She appeared in the blink of an eye; then left quickly and as quietly as a mouse.

MAGIC OF LOVE

Mihovil's unexpected decision to stay overnight with me produced in me a state of delightful excitement, an overwhelming flood of emotion from my trembling heart. I was watching him sitting in a velvet armchair while the dark night interwoven with the threads of moonlight unfolded, enticing us into its bower.

There was a reflection of the candle's flame flickering in his eyes, full of longing for the silent delight that, like a whisper of the soul, made no words necessary. The slightly crossed black eye was wandering over my body penetrating it deeply. I was thrown into his arms by some divine force. My feelings were heightened, tuned to finer vibrations that transformed my whole being.

Feeling the sigh from my lips, Mihovil started kissing me, touching with a flame of his heart the hidden corners of my being. I surrendered to him, wishing to drink of this cup of immense delight. While he was kissing me, I was surrendering to him more and more, feeling the trembling of his soul. His soul broke its silence, like advancing waves rising from the emotional heights of his being.

Merged together in a dazzling light, we were like seekers of our star in the wasteland of the universes. Drowning in the ocean of infinite love, we were dancing our light dance, accompanied by the fluttering string of a cosmic violin. We were rising on floating wings of pure light, reaching for the moment of ecstasy, enveloped in primal glow. And then, as if a higher truth flared before us, the cosmic serpent coiled around our hearts, and we discovered the joy of bliss. On the threshold of this endless dimension, overflowing with pristine peace, we were vibrating with the rhythm of the Universe. We then returned to the bosom of Mother Earth, weaving the healing threads of the web of light around her.

At the moment of bliss with no end, we gave ourselves up to the burst of joy that was spreading out like boundless waves into the vastness of our souls. Stunned at the marvelous feeling of the ease of life, we never thought of seeking its cause, until, wreathed with the charm of an unseen beauty, we recognized each other as ourselves, united with eternity, and we flew away, disappearing in the endless dust of the stars.

THE SECRET SOCIETY

Alka was waiting for me in front of the Municipal Loggia, punctual as usual. She looked so beautiful this morning in a white knit dress that emphasized her waist and a wide-brimmed hat – a totally different style from the ones she used to wear. I didn't ask her why she got dressed up. We had a tacit agreement not to ask for such details.

"Dear Antonija, so much happened since we last saw each other. I couldn't wait to hear everything." Alka turned to me and hugged me.

I put my arm around her shoulders and unlocked the door. The atmosphere of the spacious hall was filled with the sanctity of silence. A temple-like atmosphere was created by the monumental sculpture of a Roman emperor, left here until the permanent exhibition of Antiques at the Archaeological Museum[22] was set up.

---

[22] The Archaeological Museum in Zadar was founded in 1832 making it the second oldest museum in Croatia and one of the oldest in this part of Europe.

Alka almost snagged it with her purse, making the steel wire, to which the statue was fastened, swing. I passed it by without batting an eye, being afraid of knocking it down. I hurried to our room where the book in a small glass cabinet was waiting for us.

"I don't know where to start," I said, unlocking the cabinet. I took the book and handed it to Alka.

Alka sat. She frowned slightly, blowing off a fine layer of dust. Then she started leafing through the pages. When she looked at the first half of the book, she raised her head to look for her cellphone in her purse. She dialed a number and said that she would cancel the lunch set for today.

I looked at Alka inquisitively. She said, "Nothing serious; just another one that wouldn't last. It's for sure different with you."

"I don't know what to say. After this book appeared, nothing was the same."

"I don't doubt it. It's really an extraordinary book. But, what about love? I am awfully curious. Would you let your girlfriend break our silent agreement for awhile?"

"Well, what's the point in keeping a secret? It was love at first sight: a sacred, transformative feeling, a unifying power thanks to which you exist, thanks to which you recognize yourself in others and others in you. It wove a thrilling spell around me and filled my heart with passion. I never had such a relationship. I am afraid to lose it. Please don't ask me more because there is nothing else I can tell you."

"Oh, you really made my day. It will be easier for me to get on with the work! I won't ask you anything more. The glimmer of inner flame in your eyes says it all," Alka responded delightedly.

I smiled and said in return, "Let's start."

"It won't be easy. It will take a long time to decipher the text," said Alka pensively.

"We can handle it. It's important to start and then help will come."

"Take some money out of my purse. We should celebrate this solemn moment. Could I buy you lunch?" Alka said, assuming an air of importance. "And now, to work," she continued seriously, becoming absorbed in reading.

When I came back from a nearby restaurant with some fragrant food, I found Alka in a pile of papers writing something. She looked at me, adjusting her lavender cat glasses. Then she said, "Unbelievable, they repeat at regular intervals!"

I approached her and took a closer look. She showed me some abstract signs in the text. They seemed to appear as some kind of a space between words. From whichever side she started counting, she couldn't group them together properly until, in one place, a strange symbol appeared. It was reversed, imprinted on the back of the book. It was obvious that it was an initial capital letter shaped like a snake tail.

"Alka, you wouldn't believe it," I turned to her excitedly as I turned the first page of the book with embossed initials, with the two snake-like tail-shaped letters "L", outlined in golden threads.

"A Secret Society?" Alka looked at me questioningly then bit off a piece of pizza. "I couldn't explain it any other way."

"On the island? Though, as we know, there used to be pre-Christian shrines along the islands on the Adriatic Sea where pagan rituals were performed. But I couldn't associate them with the grandmother Lucija."

"We don't know what our ancestors were doing," Alka added. "Wait," she said and started turning the pages. "Antonija, it will take a few hours. Go home."

"I will stay with you."

"As you wish. Get some pizza and treat yourself."

I stayed with Alka, counting pages. Toward evening, when it got darker, Alka lifted her head from the book and asked, "How many pages?"

"One hundred."

"Humph, it's interesting that each new chapter

begins with seven snake-like tail symbolical signs. I
don't know if I can decipher them."

"Leave that for now. That is enough for today."

"Yes, you were right, Antonija. Mihovil will be
with us next weekend. It will be easier."

"I hope," I said pensively. He had not crossed
my mind the entire day. It could only be attributed
to the book.

THE END OF THE weekend approached, but Mihovil
didn't appear. He called me late Friday night, apologiz-
ing. I wasn't upset, as I knew that he always had a lot
of work to do at the Faculty of Philosophy. I was more
concerned about whether Alka would have enough
time to finish the project quickly. But I shouldn't have
worried about that. Alka was sitting in the library from
early Saturday morning onward. There was no progress in the work until late afternoon when I met Dr.
Sandalic in the hall. Lost in his thoughts, as usual, he
walked right past me without even noticing me. Only
after I called him silently, he coughed, feeling uncomfortable and noticing me. He asked me, "Antonija, how
is the work progressing?"

"It is going slowly. We obtained some insights, but
it would be premature to draw any firm conclusions."

"May I see it?"

"You are welcome to see it. Let's go."

We entered the room, quietly knocking at the door. Alka had her head buried in a book, sitting in a deep spiritual, contemplative pose. She moved away from the book, hearing Dr. Sandalic's greetings.

"I am glad that this magnificent work is in your hands." He shook her hand and introduced himself, "Dr. Sandalic."

"Thank you. You may call me Alka," she said in return.

"Dr. Sandalic wanted to see whether we were making progress. Could you explain this to him briefly?"

"It is hard to say anything. The book is possibly written in a coded script to conceal some secret knowledge. Knowing the structure of the paper would be helpful."

"I know a top expert in forensic archeology from the Institute of Forensic Medicine and Criminology from the Medical Faculty of Split[23]. Let me know if you wish to contact him."

"Hopefully it won't be necessary," I said and turned toward Alka. "Let's go, Alka, you look tired."

"Well, it's time to go," Dr. Sandalic shook my hand.

---

[23] The Medical Faculty of Split was founded in 1997 as a part of the University of Split.

He said good-bye to Alka and left.

"Yes, it's time," Alka said. Then she grabbed her purse and gave me a sign to get her white silk scarf with silver sequins tied around the back of my chair.

"It's gorgeous. It's sparkling like the shiny moonlight."

"I may need it. They forecast that the north wind may develop into a storm toward evening."

"I am afraid it's dark already," I answered anxiously.

"We stayed too long," Alka looked at her watch and gave a nod of assent. "See you tomorrow. I will call you if I need you."

"Yes, sure," I said and turned toward the City Watch[24].

---

[24] The clock tower of the 16th century City Guard on the opposite side of the City Loggia is located on the People's Square (Croatian: Narodni trg) in Zadar.

THE AWAKENING

Sunday flew by. Alka didn't call until evening. She called when I was about to unlock my Smart car and go downtown.

"Antonija, could you come and meet me now?" Alka said to me excitedly.

"I will be there in a moment," I answered and started my car.

As I arrived at the Municipal Loggia, the clock on the City Tower struck seven. I ran to the room where Alka was. I didn't knock on the door. The door was half-open. I stood for a while with my mouth open, not uttering a word.

"Come in, Antonija," Alka said to me, calmly. Illuminated by the candlelight, she was leafing through the pages, writing down some hieroglyphs.

"What are you doing? You could burn the book!" I yelled and ran towards Alka, wanting to grab the candle out of her hands.

"Come closer and take a look!" Alka said as she

pulled my arm. Then she touched the backside of the page with her fingertips. It was that same page with a reversed, strange snake-like tail-shaped symbol.

"Unbelievable! You are a natural sorceress!" I cried tears of joy and kissed Alka on her cheek which was flushed from the warmth of the candle.

"It is written in ritual symbols. I think that a particular succession of syllables and intervals reproduces meditative mantra chanting. But I cannot decipher the script," Alka said, excitement in her voice.

"How did you come up with that old method?" I asked. Then I heard a voice coming from the entrance.

"Mihovil?" I gave an exclamation.

"You will burn the book," Mihovil said in a loud voice and took the candle. He started moving it lightly over the back of the page until the text didn't appear.

"Naga Shakti," I mumbled silently. I continued uttering the ritual mantra, laying my fingers on the neck of the candle. I was uttering it faster and faster when I suddenly began to sway, and I lost my balance.

I instantaneously found myself out of my body. Drifting in a powerful energy whirlpool, I flew up to the window. It seemed as though I was separated from open space by an invisible thread. I knew I wouldn't come back if I stepped over its edge. Somewhere from the distance, from the threshold of infinity, Mihovil's face was smiling at me. He was enveloped by a dazzling corona of light. I was soaking up its rays, pulsating in the rhythm of the Universe. I was almost immersed in peace when I saw another face. I shuddered, seeing a dark shadow enveloping Mihovil. It looked like his projected body. I screamed out of fear for Mihovil to blow out the candle. The shadow vanished in the blink of an eye. It seemed to me that it vanished into a parallel dimension when I returned slowly back into my body.

All of this happened in seconds. Although I couldn't remember it anymore, it radically changed my perception of reality. It was some kind of an awakening of spiritual identity. That it wasn't just my imagination I understood from Mihovil's eyes. They were sparkling with love.

Then I heard voices, one after the other, more and more voices, voices from the otherworldly spaces that were re-echoing the tones of the etheric music of the spheres.

"Antonija, you have gained the powers, the royal Naga powers! You have achieved unity within yourself and with everything!"

"Naga Shakti," I uttered silently and shut the book.

WHEN THE MAGIC IS GONE

O n Friday night the phone rang. On the other end of the line I heard the excited tone of Dr. Sandalic's voice, instead of the voice I was expecting.

"Antonija, we have to meet. Could you come to the library?"

"But it's already nine o'clock." I couldn't hide my restlessness.

"Antonija, please, I'll be waiting at the same place in the hall."

As I approached the entrance, I saw Dr. Sandalic standing in the hall, staring at a marble Roman bust. The statue, representing the wife of the Roman emperor, was soon to be relocated to the Archeological Museum.

"Elegant like this sleeping diva," Dr. Sandalic approached me, keeping his eye on the bust of the Roman goddess. "Let's go, Antonija."

The whiff of mystery that was hanging over the

marble bust only intensified the feeling of spiteful solitude that was following me. As I entered the room, I couldn't restrain myself, "Dr. Sandalic, what do you want to tell me?"

"Calm down, Antonija," Dr. Sandalic gently put his arm across my shoulders. Then, he seated me on the chair. "When did you see Mihovil last time?"

"On Sunday night. Alka called and I went to the library. Why do you ask?"

"Antonija, on Monday morning, the day after your meeting with Alka, I stopped by the library to see if the book was in its place. I found Mihovil with his head buried in a book. It was weird seeing him there because he should have been in Zagreb already. I haven't seen him since then."

It's strange that he hasn't called me, I thought to myself. Then, a sense of foreboding came over me.

"I was looking for him today at the Faculty of Philosophy. He should have held his lecture in the morning. He disappeared without a trace; even his professor doesn't know where he is. Now, the librarian Milica found this, this morning." Dr. Sandalic paused, then he opened the book and there was a page torn from the book.

The page with the ritual mantras, I said to myself.

"He left this for us," Dr. Sandalic handed me a note

with a trembling hand. I read in disbelief, "Clear the name of the ancient Liburnians!"

"What could it mean? I cannot believe that he tore the page out. Ritual mantras are an important part of the text. Mihovil wouldn't do that," I cried out.

"I'll find out what happened. I'll look for him," Dr. Sandalic said with a booming voice. Before he ran toward the door, he turned to me and said, "Let me know if Mihovil calls you."

"Yes, absolutely," I said in return.

THE DAYS THAT FOLLOWED were melancholy ones, a dull pain wound around the soul. Mihovil didn't come. The room where he kissed me the last time was dead calm. It was filled with the intoxicating sweet scent of love that left a wistful fragrance in my hair.

I was fantasizing about his touches, his kisses with a mild taste of sea salt. I couldn't understand how he could vanish just like that without a trace. What had made him go off on his own and disappear like a shadow?... When I thought of him, I felt a strange restless feeling. I wanted it to fade away with the whistling wind and put my soul back on the path of happiness.

I was seeing Mihovil as more beautiful, dazzling and alluring than ever. His image was following me like a shadow on the gloomy walls of my room. The very idea that he was younger than I aroused in me dammed up passion. I imagined his slender body, his silky soft, gentle hands. He was focusing his sad, slightly crossed black eye on me, in which I glimpsed a look of longing. It flickered like a candle flame, gently caressing my bosom.

I couldn't separate myself from being in his presence. I wished to throw myself into his embrace, catch a glimmer of the bliss that he lavished upon me. But soon the longing would be overshadowed by somber melancholy, hopeless pain caused by his absence. I tried to send it away by replacing it with dreamlike visions created by the imagination, remembering moments when our hearts were crying with joy.

The whirl of passion soon became too strong for the heart to endure. It became an ardent flicker and, in time, faded away, though there was a glimmer of hope that I would see Mihovil again and indulge in the enchantment of love.

THE SEARCH

I t has been a long time since the occurrence of the fantastic events in Zadar, and Mihovil's sudden disappearance. Life has gone on as usual. I enjoyed a two-week trip to Split to the Faculty of Medicine. There I worked with students and did various activities in which I became so engrossed that I almost forgot about Mihovil. Until... one night in June, Dr. Sandalic called. We agreed to meet at the beginning of the week at the Faculty of Philosophy.

Usually punctual, but this time I was a little late for the meeting. I couldn't find a suitable dress with the right color to match my blue patent-leather purse. In the end I picked my light blue Chanel suit which showed off my fine figure for a woman in her early forties.

Professor Sandalic got confused when he saw me since he was not expecting to see me so well-dressed. He turned to me and said politely, "You look nice, Antonija."

"Thank you." I gave him a restrained smile, then looked away to the framed diploma that adorned the worn-out wall of the faculty room. A low, kind voice interrupted my thoughts. It inspired fatherly confidence.

"Antonija, there is no trace of Mihovil."

"Yes, unfortunately," I said in return.

The thought of Mihovil almost made me cry. I was pondering the streams of anxious thoughts looking for the answer, "Why?"

Doctor Sandalic looked at me; then he adjusted his pince-nez that was clumsily hooked at the edge of his nose, "Antonija, it is not an easy matter. There is something you should know," he added. "Mihovil's father, a renowned linguist, Dr. Luka Dorcic, had been under surveillance by the secret police. He probably fell into their hands and was killed. He supposedly strayed too much off course in his research of early Croatian ethnogenesis."

"Yes, I know an area of his special concern was the Non-Slavic origin of Croatians," I responded, collecting myself for awhile at the very mention of this theme. "What does it have to do with the book?" I continued in a serious tone.

"Well, modern Croatians are an ancient maritime nation. This is supported by the theory according to which our ancestors, early Liburnians, arrived around the 11th and 12th centuries B.C. from the shores of the Levant[25] to the Adriatic Sea. The newest biogenetic research confirms the link to the Levant as well."

"The book most likely dates from the Middle Ages. Where do you see the link?"

"Likewise, the island legends in the archaic Chakavian dialect that have been preserved in the northern Adriatic tell of the maritime migration of the nations from the east. They are the link to the Vedic[26] linguistic heritage of Croatians. Mihovil's father was studying them."

"Certainly Mihovil mentioned an archaic dialect, although there is no confirmation that the book was really written in it."

"Mihovil was keenly interested in the book. He wanted to settle his father's estate. The indications that I have show that in the quest of the original script he went in the direction of the ancient Levant."

"I couldn't believe he was gone, just like that! Maybe we should call the police."

---

[25] The Levant is a geographical area that refers to the Eastern shore of the Mediterranean which is now Israel, part of Syria, Lebanon, and Western Jordan.

[26] Vedic – relating to the Vedas. The Vedas are a collection of sacred texts originating in ancient India. They are a treasure trove of timeless wisdom and one of the oldest scriptures in the world.

"Antonija, I would leave the police alone for now. Mihovil's family is dogged by their inglorious past, and a troubled relationship with the authorities. I already mentioned that his father was under surveillance by the secret police. He probably fell into their hands and was killed. You know that scientists who promote nonstandard, scientific methods are closely followed by the secret police."

Yes, it's possible, I said to myself, thinking how Dr. Sandalic, feeling the tragedy of Mihovil's family, wanted to find him desperately. His father's work was surely an important link for decoding the text of the book and the early history of Croatians.

Doctor Sandalic coughed lightly, then continued, "You were close. If you had a chance to go for scientific training abroad at the possible place of Mihovil's abode, would you go?"

"I don't understand. What do you mean?"

Doctor Sandalic started explaining in great detail. "Mihovil has most likely joined the United Nations mission. It so happened that the Lebanese Ministry of Public Health announced vacancies last week for physicians who would willingly go to work in Lebanon.

"The Head of the Department of Clinical Psychology, Dr. Jakov Brusic, supports you wholeheartedly and agrees to give you a reference to participate in the project of mental health promotion. As an excellent psychiatrist, you have had good results with our casualties of the Croatian War of Independence[27]. You helped them not only with a classical approach to mental disorders, but with meditation techniques as well. Because of frequent warfare, they cannot cope with posttraumatic stress problems anymore and have decided to seek the help of world specialists. I think that you would be excellent for that: you are educated and talented and would be additionally motivated because of Mihovil. The only aggravating circumstance is that you may be embarking on an adventure of no return. It's dangerous there. You would need to be ready for it."

I was listening to the Professor as if I were half-asleep. Just the thought of being able to see Mihovil, the grace of my life, aroused a hidden smoldering desire in me, stirring up the old flame of love. It blazed up with the impulse of hope that breathed new life into me and I was running into Mihovil's arms, overtaken by fond memories and secret dreams. I suddenly awoke to the touch of Dr. Sandalic's hand. I said, collecting myself, "Yes, of course. You know that I would follow Mihovil anywhere."

---

[27] The war after the breakup of Yugoslavia that was fought from 1991 to 1995.

Doctor Sandalic handed me a note with a strange name, Khalil, and a cellphone number. He said that I could contact him for anything I might need. He continued, blushing slightly, "There is something else I would like to tell you. I lost the love of my life from student days. She went to Lebanon. She was a real Levantine beauty, an enchanting woman with Eastern features, a high forehead and crystal clear black eyes. Our love made me think of you. If I could turn back time, I wouldn't have let her go. Fathima was from a traditional Muslim family. She left at the demand of her father. What's done is done. I think you won't lose your love as I did."

Dr. Sandalic kissed my hand. I was about to stand up and leave, but the Professor stopped me, "Before you go, tell me honestly, do you love him?"

"Yes, yes," I answered. But how could I explain that it was something I have never felt, something beyond human power, like the love of soul mates, love for a man with whom you want to share the joy in every moment and embark on the adventure of your life.

BEIRUT
ADVENTURE

—

II

JOURNEY TO LEBANON

The *Lufthansa* jet was landing at the Beirut Rafic
Hariri International Airport. The Sun was blazing, leaving the impression that it would penetrate
through the windows with its thick rays. From my
bird's eye view, I was watching an impressive runway,
built out at sea. Its triangular geometric shape resembled the runway for spaceships.

We landed at exactly midday. I shut the book I
had been reading by British bestselling writer Robert
Fisk[28], *Pity the Nation: The Abduction of Lebanon*. I
bought it on the advice of my girlfriend before the trip
to look into the Lebanon tragedy and complete my not
so meager knowledge of the Middle East. According to
critics, the book was an excellent piece of work with a
slightly different political opinion about Lebanon than

---

[28] Robert Fisk (born 1946) is an English writer and journalist.
He holds many British and international journalism awards.
He has lived in the Arab world for more than forty years,
and since 1989 has been correspondent for *The Independent*
based in Beirut.

the one of the Middle Eastern governments, Great Britain, and its allies. With an investigative journalist's eye, the author succeeded in giving an in-depth view of Lebanese society.

I took off my monocle, and fixed my hair, pushing a thin lock of gray hair that was blurring my view off my forehead. I freshened up my reddish lipstick and found my sunglasses. I looked at the screen above the seat out of the corner of my eye and read the last instructions of the flight crew before landing. I smiled a contented smile back to a familiar face, mine. My face reminded me once again of a mature woman, who, thanks to her youthful appearance could still proudly stand out in a crowd.

Before I moved towards the exit with the other passengers, I looked for the beads in my purse. I held them in my hand against the upper part of my suit and silently prayed to the glory of Lord Shiva. I intuitively knew that luck wouldn't betray me although I had arrived right before a series of grievous events. These had started on the 12th of July when the Israeli army ambushed Lebanon from the Lebanese side of the border.

I moved through the passport control easily and then headed towards the exit out of the monumental building. I stood in front of the souvenir shop waiting for one of the Beirut medical students who was supposed to pick me up. Standing there, I glanced in the store window filled with diverse chocolate candies against a background of tiny Lebanese flags. I leafed through a tourist guidebook about Lebanon, reading how the holy cedar tree stood for different symbols in Lebanese history: the dwelling of the Gods in the Sumerian Epic of *Gilgamesh*[29] up to the Lebanon's Cedar Revolution of 2005[30].

I was so occupied with transporting myself mentally to the place where not so long ago bloody events had occurred that I almost didn't notice a young woman standing right behind me with the printed sign saying *Antonia*. She had flowing curly hair and a bronze complexion. She was beautiful, although short and a little roundish. She had short knee pants, a large belly and a button ring sticking out of her belly button. I had the thought, how could she walk dressed like that among so many Arabs. At first I couldn't determine if she was African American or Latina. It's hard to tell

---

[29] *The Epic of Gilgamesh* is an epic poem from ancient Mesopotamia that is often regarded as the oldest written story in the world. Its oldest existing versions in cuneiform script date back to the early 3rd or late 2nd millennium B.C.

[30] The Cedar Revolution of Independence started in March 2005 after the assassination of the former Lebanese Prime Minister, Rafik Hariri (1944-2005).

at first with Americans, but I realized the moment she introduced herself.

"I am Concetta, a Mexican from Texas studying in Beirut. Welcome!"

"I appreciate you meeting me here," I responded.

We went to the taxi stand where the drivers were shouting and competing among themselves to win customers. Luckily Concetta had already booked a taxi, otherwise it would be hard for us to get safely downtown.

We soon reached the luxury Hotel de Ville in the lively Sodeco[31] district near downtown Beirut. The hotel had been recently renovated and now provided comfortable luxury accommodations in their elegant, brightly painted rooms.

The taxi driver took my baggage to the entrance. I tipped him generously. He looked me up and down with his experienced eye. That was probably the reason why Concetta didn't leave my side for one minute. She walked me to my room, wishing me goodnight and a peaceful night's rest.

The room was on the seventh floor; it was my only complaint about this exceedingly

---

[31] On the corner of the East Beirut's Sodeco Square stands Beit Beirut, an imposing, neo-Ottoman style building, previously known as the Barakat building. Beit Beirut is now a museum that commemorates the Lebanese Civil War (1975-1990).

beautiful and tastefully decorated terracotta room in Mediterranean style.

I put down my bulky baggage and went towards the wide balcony, something I always do upon arrival at some renowned tourist destinations. If I hadn't found myself in one of the most dangerous cities in the world, I would have dived into the bed sheets and slept under the open sky filled with glimmering star clusters of a wide variety of colors.

I took off my high heels and gently massaged my tired feet. I didn't have the energy to unpack the baggage. I took the essential toiletry kit out and took a quick shower.

I was hoping for a comfortable bed and a good night's sleep, something I had been missing recently. I finally did manage to sleep all night, maybe because I was tired, or maybe because I was in a different environment than the one I was used to.

Thanks to a deep sleep, I was in a great mood in the morning. I didn't miss my morning prayer and prayed to the glory of Lord Shiva.

Coming downstairs to the dining hall, I saw Concetta drinking her morning coffee with a companion. She called me by waving her hand and then introduced me to the man with a familiar name, Khalil. He was the first handsome, well-mannered man that

I had met since my arrival who didn't look at me with prankish eyes, but who, to everyone's surprise, did kiss my hand.

Khalil was well-built, broad-shouldered, and had a proud bearing. He was distinguished by his mystical blue eyes and high cheekbones, which were in contrast with the features of a typical brown-eyed Arab man with an olive complexion, and a long nose. This gave him an aristocratic appearance. He wasn't very attractive, although he might capture one's attention with his stylish clothing and tactfulness.

Concetta literally gave him into my keeping; then she excused herself and took her leave. She wished me a nice time in Lebanon in the company of a loyal man and, as would be proven true, a best friend, as the name Khalil means in Arabic.

THE DAWN OF WAR

Khalil took me to the Faculty of Medicine at Beirut Arab University[32] after breakfast. We went to the office of the Eastern Mediterranean Regional Office of the World Health Organization[33] headed by Doctor Fathima. Khalil then excused himself and went out, leaving me alone in Fathima's office.

Fathima, although past her prime, was still beautiful. She had a clean-cut face, nice looking nose, full lips, and was amply endowed with a well-developed bust. Her hair was tied up in a bun and her eyes accentuated with black eyeliner. She was dressed elegantly in a stylish red short-sleeved suit. It didn't surprise me that she caught Dr. Sandalic's eye. In short, she was a real, Oriental beauty.

---

[32] Beirut Arab University, established in 1960 is a Lebanese private university and one of the leading higher education institutions in the Arab Region.

[33] The World Health Organization is an agency of the United Nations that is concerned with international public health. It was established in 1948 and its headquarter is in Geneva, Switzerland.

"Dear Antonija, please have a seat."

"Thank you."

"I was expecting you. I am not sure if Matija told you about our relationship. We were intimate friends long ago. We have stayed good friends. It looks like you were very motivated to come to find your love. I'll help you as much as I can. I represent the Eastern Mediterranean Office of the World Health Organization. We need a reliable person from a region affected by war who could not only provide medical care to our suffering people, but give spiritual comfort as well. I remembered Matija and asked him for someone suitable and here you are, Antonija. I believe that you are worthy of the task and will see it through."

A series of loud explosions suddenly interrupted Fathima's speech. I didn't pay any attention to it, thinking that it was quite normal for Beirut. A short time later the phone rang and I couldn't communicate with Fathima anymore. The startled look on her face gave the impression that she had just heard some disturbing news. Her abrupt hand gesture signaled that the meeting was over for the day. She excused herself and set out for a meeting at the Ministry of Health.

In front of Fathima's office, Khalil was sitting patiently. The restrained expression on his face suddenly changed when a much louder explosion reverberated. He grabbed his cellphone and called a taxi that would take me to the hotel. He spoke to me in a serious tone and said he would call me in the evening.

Upon arrival at the hotel, I went directly to my room. I ordered a meal; then took a shower and fell asleep. Late at night a knock on the door woke me up. I heard Khalil's voice and put my robe on. I wasn't expecting him at the hotel room door. He was remarkably elegant in a fashionable suit in the same color that matched his sky blue eyes. The scowl on his face that I had noticed in the morning had disappeared. He was smiling, showing pure white teeth as if he could clear away the moment of unease with his smile. Then he kissed me on my cheek. I could smell a strong fragrance of a perfume that was in total contrast with his sophisticated appearance, and that gave me the impression of a macho type man. Watching him, I thought he must have had a good reason to wear such perfume. I was not expecting that he would invite me to go out.

I went to the bathroom and changed into sweatpants and a V-neck T-shirt.

"Humph," Khalil said, "couldn't you put on something more suitable and feminine? I am taking you out to dinner."

"Yes, certainly."

I chose a black knee-length low-cut evening gown. Not only did it emphasize my femininity, but every time I wore it, it drew men's eyes. Since I didn't want to attract too much attention, I put on my silk scarf embellished with silver threads.

"Not a word," added Khalil, discreetly lowering his gaze to my shoulders.

We took Khalil's Grand Cherokee jeep towards West Beirut and the American University. It was located in the vicinity of Sheikh Mankoush Club. It wasn't only a restaurant but one of the city's best known gay clubs.

I was expecting Khalil would take me to an elegant restaurant. I was perplexed, and didn't feel like having dinner. I ordered only orange juice. I was sitting listlessly watching the club's guests in astonishment; they didn't look particularly like gay community members to me. Khalil turned to me, knowing well what was going through my mind.

"Antonija, I know what has crossed your mind. I am not gay, although I have many respected friends among them. We came here for a reason. There are not many safe places to go out in Beirut. For everyone here, I am a gay man in the company of an attractive woman. That way we draw less attention."

I responded with a sigh of relief, nodding assent,

"I didn't doubt you although you are unusually mysterious and not very inclined to reveal the reason why you have been following me from the very beginning."

"Antonija, you arrived on the 12th of July, the day when the armed conflict started with Israel. It may develop into a full scale war at any moment. It's getting dangerous on the streets of Beirut. The fact that you are a foreign citizen makes things more difficult, though a mitigating circumstance might be that you are a well-respected specialist. Moreover, you came at the invitation of Dr. Fathima Fakhri, our leading public health expert.

"Antonija, I would like to discuss some details about your personal life. I think about your would-be partner Mihovil, who disappeared without trace in Croatia. It seems that he arrived in Lebanon and likely joined the United Nations mission. A young colleague from Doctors Without Borders[34] thinks he saw him a few weeks ago at the lecture of the famous professor Noam Chomsky[35] at the American University of

---

[34] Doctors Without Borders is an international, humanitarian, medical, non-profit organization founded by doctors and journalists in 1971 in France.

[35] Noam Chomsky (born 1928) is an American linguist, philosopher, cognitive scientist, historian, social critic and political activist. He is considered the father of modern linguistics.

Beirut[36]. We are investigating if he is still in Beirut or has left the country."

"I don't know any more than you, and I don't know much about you," I responded coldly. I was watching Khalil carefully while reclining in the armchair. Deep lines in the corner of his eyes were giving him a stern expression. He looked at me blankly, though his tense pose indicated that he wasn't completely calm. My keen woman's eye couldn't help but notice his hidden interest in me as a woman. He reminded me for a moment of a police investigator who is just pretending to be someone else. His aristocratic features bore a suggestion of a refined expression. There was nothing resembling a policeman. I was hoping that he would tell me more about Mihovil.

Khalil interrupted my train of thought.

"Antonija, you were committed to my care at the request of Dr. Fathima Fakhri. Her longtime friend, your colleague, Dr. Sandalic, expressed his concern about Mihovil's disappearance. We are trying to figure out where we lost his trail. You can trust me."

Then I responded more warmly, "I don't know why, but I trust you."

Khalil looked back and continued, "There is

---

[36] A private university founded in 1866, one of the most prestigious universities in the Middle East.

something else. The situation is difficult because of political tensions. I don't know if you heard that Hezbollah militants[37], who are reportedly controlled by Iran, captured two Israeli soldiers today with the intent to kill the others. People wonder if Israel will bomb Lebanon which could start a war."

Indeed, looking in the direction of TV screens on high stands at different locations in the room, I saw people hanging out and listening in disbelief about the newest events.

Khalil stood up and lifted his glass of whisky.

"Cheers, Antonija! From now on I'll keep a vigilant eye on you and I am taking you under my protection."

"Cheers," I said in response.

I understood Khalil's desire to relax for a while with a little alcohol. He was usually so considerate, but didn't offer me a drink. He could probably tell from my surprised look that I don't drink alcohol.

I stole a glance at him, wrapped up in thought, as I asked myself whether he brought me here to find out more about Mihovil. Or maybe he hoped to find him here. In a gay club? It was the last thing in the world I could have imagined.

Soft music was playing in the bar, in Khalil's opinion, one of the best in Beirut. I surrendered

---

[37] A Shia militant group based in Lebanon.

to the gentle chords, silently sitting in the private dining-room not exchanging a single word. It was almost eleven when I thought that I heard louder and louder explosions in the distance. Khalil woke up instantaneously from a doze. He left a tip for the waiter, quickly grabbed my hand and took me to the car.

All the way home the radio was quietly playing. After the monotonous jazz bar music, Norah Jones[38] was a breath of fresh air. I kept listening in silence. With moonlight and a handful of brilliant stars, the view of the sky would have made the atmosphere warmer if the power hadn't suddenly failed in the surrounding area, as we were approaching the out-skirts of West Beirut. Khalil quickly stepped on the gas. We drove as quickly as lightning, leaving behind us a spectral image of the city in the night.

We arrived just before the hotel was closed for the night. Khalil hugged me. He whispered in my ear that everything would be all right if I stayed in the hotel room until his next call. He gave me another cellphone just in case and asked me to use only it from now on.

Extremely tired I dove into bed fully dressed and fell asleep. That night I had my first dream about Mihovil after his disappearance. Only love could

---

[38] Norah Jones (born 1979) is an American singer, songwriter, and pianist. She has won nine Grammy Awards.

have let my imagination roam to such an extent as I drifted off to sleep reviving the ancient Anzotika, the Liburnian Goddess of Love, who would take me through the Levant in search of happiness.

I wished to seize the moment of bliss just to remember Mihovil's touch. At that moment, the Goddess Anzotika gave me the experience of it. She provided me abundantly with everything that reminded me of our time together: I could catch the sound of the sea imbued with the scent of salt and native land. I could feel Mihovil's presence in the air. I wished he would kiss me just one more time so that I could enjoy the taste of the sea salt on his lips. Flooded with perfect happiness, I dove into his embrace. I was diving deeper and deeper, and would have become lost in his embrace when I suddenly realized that maybe the day of our last meeting was near. I didn't want to believe it. I was looking for a way to push away the unwanted thoughts. Then I heard the ritual mantra from the book of grandmother Lucija. The sound was coming from everywhere and, carried by its power, I wished to leap over time. I wished to step into eternity and stay in that beautiful dream that would bind me forever with Mihovil and the enchanting scent of love.

THE MORNING EXPLOSION

Somewhere around ten in the morning, I suddenly heard a strong explosion which made the earth tremble and the windows rattle. I woke up shaken and sat straight up in bed. I ran toward the TV to turn it on when the phone rang. I heard Khalil telling me to go to the balcony. From there, a big cloud of smoke was spreading in the distance. He stated that the Beirut Rafic Hariri International Airport was just bombed by Israeli aircraft. Fortunately, I trusted him. Otherwise, I couldn't have stood the pressure. I stayed in the hotel, not leaving my room for two days. I wanted to dispel my claustrophobic fear through meditation, but I was not able to overcome it until after a good, light, vegetarian, maritime lunch.

I spent the rest of the day thinking about everything that had happened to me the last few days. But thinking of how to find Mihovil occupied my mind so much that I completely forgot about the scary news reports on increasingly dangerous events.

It was about six in the late afternoon when I was preparing to meditate. I had left the TV on all day. When I went to turn it off, I saw on the screen the latest reports of the Israeli bombing of southern Lebanon. These were the decisive events that would lead up to the war of an uncertain end.

There was no word from Khalil. The TV was my only connection to the outside world and that was barely working, thanks to the hotel generator. The hotel personnel were helpful as much as they could be. They didn't want to stir up any fuss, most likely by order of the city authorities.

I tried to fall asleep in the evening, but I managed it only just before dawn. I awoke after about half an hour startled by the sound of an explosion. I recognized the sound of a bomber. Then silence fell. It was perhaps the most frightening moment of silence, bitterness and suspense of my life. After about ten minutes, a muezzin[39] broke the silence with his prayer from the nearby minaret of one of the downtown mosques. My answer to the prayer was to quickly grab the beads out of my purse and start praying the prayer to the glory of Lord Shiva. Feeling exhausted, I finally fell asleep.

I had a significant dream. The Goddess Sentona the Liburnian Goddess of Beauty and Fertility and

[39] Muezzin, Ar. – a man who calls Muslims to prayer.

patroness of travelers, bestowed Her grace on me. When she approached me, I could feel Her gentleness. She was radiating an all-pervading peace. I entered the Spiral Vortex and experienced Goddess energy, and was carried away by the magical dance of the Universe. Through the Goddess energy, I discovered the eternal beauty which enlivened the Goddess within. I realized that I have to live daily in the flow of the Goddess energy and spread love to receive it myself and enjoy divine protection.

IT WAS ALREADY LATE morning when a squeaky entrance door suddenly woke me up. I rubbed my sleepy eyes and put on my silk scarf that I had left on the back of the chair after coming back from dinner with Khalil. I approached the table and noticed the Shiva prayer beads near the telephone receiver. At first, it didn't seem strange to me to think that I had left them there yesterday and carelessly forgotten them. Then, I bit my lip, knowing that it couldn't be because I had fallen asleep holding them. Fear gripped me completely when I opened the closet and spotted my suitcase with my clothes all jumbled up. I went to the bathroom where I left my purse and found it open, hanging on the rack in the same place where I had left it. I hurriedly began pulling out cosmetics. When I opened my wallet, I was relieved to see that all the documents were in their place. Then Khalil's cellphone rang. I frantically grabbed the cellphone and yelled, "Khalil!"

"That's me, sweetheart."

Khalil's voice eased my mind. He said he was coming to pick me up in about half an hour. When he came, I ran into his arms and kissed him joyously. I hadn't felt such joy in quite a long time. He convinced me that such searches are routine for Beirut. I wasn't sure if I could trust him. His behavior seemed unusual. Seeming cool-headed, he grabbed the cellphone and began dialing. I didn't understand what he was saying because he was speaking Arabic. I could tell from the tone of his voice that he wasn't talking to the police. I thought it didn't seem important anymore because of the wartime circumstances. He told me to pack up as we were going to the mountains for the weekend.

We went quickly down to the hotel lobby. Khalil called a taxi. It took us to an isolated place on the outskirts of the city. From there we headed in Khalil's Grand Cherokee jeep straight for the Shouf mountains and the village of Keyfoun[40] above Beirut. I fell asleep

[40] A village in the Shouf mountains above Beirut, the capital of Lebanon, with a stunning view of Beirut and the Mediterranean Sea.

in the car feeling peaceful in Khalil's company. I awoke to the news from the German Embassy on the car radio. They were informing people that the road to Damask was reduced to rubble. Lebanon was cut-off from the rest of the world and the only safe passage was to the north. I was relieved by the news that they had put me on the waiting list for the evacuation with other foreign citizens. However, I wouldn't have felt so enthusiastic if I had known that Khalil had a different plan in mind.

IN KEYFOUN, TAKING A BREAK FROM BEIRUT EXPLOSIONS

Sitting comfortably in a soft antique chair covered with white satin, I was observing Khalil in disbelief, asking myself how almost in the midst of war I found myself in such a royally furnished home, in a beautiful spacious room, with a view of a pine forest that descended steeply down to the sea. I observed elegant, brown curtains that dropped heavily to the marble floor while framing a tall wide crown pine tree imposingly rising above the open terrace.

After repeated explosions there was a brief silence, broken by the barely audible murmur of rain. I wanted to feel the soft patter of rain and sip a few drops from the fragrant pine needles. Khalil interrupted my thoughts.

"What are you thinking about, Antonija?"

"May I go out to the terrace?"

"It's not a good idea. Stay inside where you are safe."

"Of course. Maybe we are protected by the National Guard. It's hard to believe that someone could own such a luxurious house that mere mortals couldn't even dream of."

"Antonija, I'll explain everything. I am a retired officer of the Lebanese Air Force."

"Retired? You look too young to be retired."

"Although officially retired, I could still do certain jobs if they called me. I am from a wealthy Shia family."

"Muslim?"

"On my paternal side I am Shiite[41] and on my maternal side Christian Maronite[42]. I have an Islamic upbringing, but I belong to Christ with all my heart."

"Interesting."

"Yes, it is, although there are more important themes to talk about. The situation is more serious than it looks. Stay with me. Refugees might need you. They will be here any minute. My personal experience tells me that they are coming at a fast pace."

"Yes, surely. I'll do my best. I won't disappoint you," I said.

---

[41] A Shiite – a Muslim of the Shia branch of Islam.

[42] Lebanese Christian Maronites are affiliated with one of the Syriac Eastern Catholic Churches.

"I have no doubt," Khalil nodded assent. Then, he went to the small precious antique cabinet. He poured a glass of whiskey from a crystal pitcher. He looked at me with a questioning look and I raised my hand as a sign that I don't drink. He drained it in one gulp. Obviously in a good mood, he walked me to my bedroom on the other side of the spacious house. He kissed me on my forehead and said goodnight.

I dropped my hand luggage, put my jewelry on the night table, and took off my shoes. I didn't have enough energy to go to the bathroom. I sprawled out on the elegant, canopied bed and felt like a princess. I fell asleep quickly not waiting for the midnight church bells to ring from the distant church bell tower. The bells announced the arrival of the first refugees.

Khalil let me sleep until lunchtime. He knocked on my door at about noon wishing me good morning. He was wearing an apron, covered with flour, clumsily put on and tied haphazardly.

"Antonija, breakfast is ready." Khalil turned to me cheerfully.

I stretched, peering out of the fragrant bed linen.

"I am coming," I said readily.

When I came downstairs to the dining hall, I was pleasantly surprised by the nicely set table. Khalil greeted me with an appetizing breakfast. The fig pastries looked as though prepared by a master chef. I asked Khalil where he learned to cook.

He said with an undertone of unease, "My wife taught me."

"Are you married?"

"I am widowed. My wife died of breast cancer six months ago."

"I am sorry."

I spoke softly, feeling deep compassion towards this wonderful man with whom I somehow shared a similar, lonesome fate. I remembered Mihovil for a moment. I was wondering if he was thinking about me at all.

Khalil's eyes were full of tears. "She was like you, Antonija: well-built, with big black eyes and beautiful curly hair. Looking at you, I am not sure if I am looking at her raised from the dead. But life goes on and I have to get used to the solitude."

"I don't know what to say. I sincerely share in your grief."

I felt in a way incredibly close to him, but I instantaneously pushed away the thought of really getting close to him. Lovers simply don't hold space for someone else in their hearts. Khalil probably felt the same way interrupting my train of thought.

"It is more than likely that I wouldn't bring my Hanna back, but you can bring back your love."

"I believe I will."

I was quite honest, although I didn't believe it completely. I wanted my memories to fade away. I wanted to occupy my mind with something else. The refugees would be here any hour now. Maybe it would be an opportunity to calm down my inner turmoil and open myself to God's love so I could share it with the ones who needed it most.

IT WAS LATE AFTERNOON, and getting dark when I heard the sound of a car. Soon after, voices reverberated from the front part of the house. I left my room and went downstairs to greet the newcomers.

Khalil introduced me to a young man with a gentle disposition and big, green eyes. You could tell he was an American by his accent. Jan was working as the representative of the United Nations-run school[43] at the Shatila[44] Palestinian refugee camp. He came

---

[43] The school run by the United Nations Relief and Work Agency for Palestinian Refugees (UNRWA) that was established in 1949.

[44] A refugee camp in Beirut, called "little Palestine" was set up by the International Committee of the Red Cross in 1949 as a

from the Keyfoun Refugee Reception Center with a little boy named Akmed. They were supposed to stay in the village waiting for their turn to embark with a convoy of refugees in a few days. Khalil was happy to give them shelter.

A small-boned, handsome, dark-complexioned boy with chestnut eyes was looking at me with a sad expression as if my own sadness was reflected in them. I felt helpless as I used to feel working with our casualties of the Croatian War of Independence. I eventually realized that giving consolation to them wasn't sufficient. I hoped it would be different with Akmed. The gap that was left in my weeping soul could have only been filled by selfless love. Maybe Akmed could be the one who could help it awaken.

Khalil invited Jan and Akmed to join us for dinner. He invited them to sit at a nearby table next to which Akmed put his small backpack. While Khalil was making dinner in the kitchen, I was carefully listening to Jan.

He was telling how he came to the Shatila Palestinian refugee camp in southern Beirut a month before the assassination of the Lebanese prime minister in February 2005. Shatila, like its wretched country Lebanon, was marked by violence and

temporary space for the Palestinian refugees.

madness. The well-known massacre in Shatila and a neighboring camp Sabra was perpetrated by a Lebanese Christian militia, the Phalangists, under the watchful eye of Israeli troops in 1982. An armed conflict is actively going on there. In such soulless places, you could meet blank-faced, unfortunate residents, conditioned by hopelessness and suffering. You couldn't even get a smile out of a child's face with toys or candy given in secret. They would look at you blankly hiding fear.

Akmed was born as the only child in the family six years ago in camp Shatila. His parents at 24 years old decided to have him despite poverty and hardships. They were born in the camp on the very day of the 1982 massacre. Their miserable fate certainly left an imprint on their child's development. Although, according to Jan, Akmed was different from any other child he had worked with at the United Nations-run school in Shatila. Akmed was the only child with a bright expression on his face, showing positive signs and interests in the world and life around him. His eyes had radiated calmness and a deep glow up until recently when the war hovered over Beirut. Jan would complete his mandate this year. He decided to take Akmed with him to the United States and show him a better part of the world. The Israeli attack was the last straw. He wanted to take Akmed with him to have a better future than his parents would have.

Jan finished his story just as Khalil brought an armful of nutritious, tasteful dishes. He certainly wanted to please Akmed by showing his love with a nice gesture.

There was a variety of green vegetables and pastries on the table. I especially enjoyed the spinach feta mini rolls with Lebanese bread. Akmed enjoyed this traditional Middle East hummus meal. He was eating decently, not wanting to show how hungry he was. When Khalil brought date filled cookies with rose water for dessert, Akmed raised the corners of his mouth into a shy smile. He started eating the cookies quickly as if he couldn't restrain himself. He ate the whole batch of them, getting powdered sugar on his cheeks.

Little heart, I said to myself, keeping my eye on the little boy's dirty cheeks. Akmed was looking at me cheerfully with his big chestnut eyes. I thought he must have been tired and it was time for him to go to bed. I told him, "Come, I'll show you where you can take a bath."

Before taking a bath, Akmed went to the table where he had left his backpack. He took out his clean clothes and went to the bathroom.

I started to clear the table when a book peeking out of the open backpack attracted my attention. I went closer and read the title: Elias Khoury[45]: *Gate of the Sun*.

"The book is about Shatila," I heard Jan telling me.

"Excuse me for my indiscretion," I said.

"It doesn't matter. If you wish you can read it. I'll leave it with you until our departure."

Still impressed by what I had heard about the refugees, I hurried to read at least a few pages before Akmed returned from the bathroom. I opened the first page, catching a glimpse of an indistinct drawing that seemed to be made by a child's hand. Leafing further, I found a page torn off the school newspaper of the United Nations-run school at the Shatila Palestinian refugee camp. I gazed at the front page photo with bated breath at two familiar crystal clear black eyes looking at me.

"Who is the man in the photo?" I cried out excitedly.

"Ishmael," I heard Akmed's voice behind me.

"Ishmael, the father of Arab nations," added Jan.

"I don't understand. Whose is this drawing? Where does this photo come from?" I asked him.

---

[45] Elias Khoury (born 1948) is a Lebanese novelist, playwright, critic, and a public intellectual.

"It's Akmed's drawing. He drew a picture of a young man who performed miracles in Shatila. He introduced himself as Ishmael. He possessed such incredible energy and the ability to heal that many were happily coming to him. The word about his abilities spread quickly, and he appeared on the front page of the school newspaper. I don't know who took his photo. I know that he kept company with the school children from the refugee camp. I haven't met him. One day he just disappeared without a trace. No one knows whether he went to the Palestinian Gaza Strip[46] or Israel."

I couldn't believe my eyes. Looking at the newspaper's photo, I was asking myself whether it was Mihovil looking at me with that same penetrating, cold, wild, maddening eye, except that the man in the picture was decisively different than the man I remembered: he wore a long white dress with a cloth wrapped around the neck and one arm, and his name tattooed on the other arm. He had an elegantly shaved beard from ear to ear, which gave him a steady and serious appearance.

---

[46] The Gaza Strip is a small Palestinian territory located along the Mediterranean coast between Egypt and Israel. It is a focal point of the Israeli-Palestinian conflict, one of the world's longest-running conflict.

Oh, my God! It couldn't be Mihovil, I thought to myself. "When did you see him last?" I turned to Jan.

"I don't remember exactly. I think it was before the Israeli attack. He was last seen with a girl of about fourteen years old. He succeeded in healing her gunshot wound fired in an accidental skirmish between Hezbollah militants. An amazing man! He didn't talk much, only to children with whom he happily played. Akmed was watching him once when he put a fellow's dislocated knee back in place. Akmed did a quick sketch of the young man. He inherited his talent from his mother who was an excellent artist. She used to organize exhibitions in the camp. The same way the young man came is the same way he disappeared, silently and unannounced. Too bad, because he was the children's favorite companion."

Khalil took the photo and said, "He is really handsome. There is unfortunately a lot of mystery regarding his movements, and honestly, I can't see my way through all this," he paused and asked me, "by the way, are you sure that the young man from the photo is your Mihovil?"

It was the last thing I wanted to hear. I stole a glance at the photo. The resemblance was striking. He looked at me with his penetrating, slightly crossed black eyes. I felt my heart tearing apart, but I didn't

want to give up. I wanted to believe that our love would
find a way out of nowhere and that my Mihovil would
appear one day.

AKMED WAS SO DIFFERENT than any other children I
had had a chance to meet. He changed my life in an
amazing way. He lit it up with hope. His pristine soul
revealed to me the majesty of God's secret. It showed
me how the spark of a genuine, God's love could only
be carried within by those pure in heart. The spark
aroused in me the feeling of the holiness of life. No
matter how far away from me Akmed might go, I knew
that the spark would continue to flame and we would
never be separated.

I composed my soul with these thoughts until
morning. I went downstairs to the dining hall around
noon, where Khalil, Jan and Akmed were finishing
their extended breakfast. I picked up a conversation
between Khalil and Jan.

"I have to leave unexpectedly for a few days for a
business trip to Beirut. Do you mind? Antonija would
keep you company. The helicopter should be here any
time now."

"To Beirut?" Jan asked him.

"Yes."

Jan paused and continued in a serious tone, "Take us with you as well. My friend called me in the morning. He received a message from the German Embassy that the first convoy to Syria is leaving on Wednesday morning. There are a few empty seats left. We'll try to embark. Please do it for the sake of this child. He deserves a better life."

"Take a break. Stay some more time with us in Keyfoun," Khalil said as he turned to Jan.

"You are a great host and I would like to stay with you," Jan said. He paused for a moment then approached Khalil. He whispered in his ear, "Who knows when our turn would come to embark on the next convoy. Akmed is leaving his homeland and his parents. I didn't tell him that he was leaving forever. Any longer stay in Lebanon would make him feel hesitant and suffer more. He has to cut ties with his parents as soon as possible in order to feel better later."

I hoped that Jan and Akmed would stay longer and that we would have a chance to get better acquainted. Hearing Jan telling Khalil to take him and Akmed with him to Beirut, I asked him pleadingly to take me as well. I wanted Akmed to be at my side. I wanted to warm his heart that was veiled in sorrow and light it up with love. Khalil eyed Jan and Akmed, then he turned his eyes on me and said decisively, "Let's go! And you too, Antonija!"

I hugged Khalil excitedly then hurried to my room to pick up the essential toiletry kit. I wore a simple skirt. I didn't have time to change clothes.

Jan and Akmed were ready to go when I came out of the house. We climbed into the green, camouflage helicopter. It seemed to me, it was the helicopter of the Lebanese Air Force.

We flew high up into the sky withdrawing rapidly from the village. We rose above the steep, serpentine road leaving behind a few houses and sparse vegetation followed by cedar and pine forests. Each of them would become less and less dense as we were approaching Beirut.

SHATILA

Amazed by the beautiful view of the Sun's disc that was standing over the sea spreading its reddish rays like a nuclear giant, I barely noticed a long line of vehicles that was climbing towards the mountains above Beirut. Khalil drew my attention to it before we started going downhill and I found myself returning to the brutal reality of life in Beirut. It was the next line of refugees who were leaving Beirut while we were approaching it, each one for reasons of their own.

We landed on the improvised airfield close to the Beirut Hippodrome. Khalil probably had a reason why he chose this place. There were two jeeps waiting for us. One of them took us back to the Hotel de Ville where I found myself again after a short absence, but this time with unexpected companions.

Khalil suddenly disappeared as usual, and then called me late at night. He told me not to leave the hotel and to spend time with Jan and Akmed. I liked their company, especially as it was getting darker and you could hear from the distance the familiar sound of increasing random explosions.

As in the days before, I managed to get up around lunchtime. The hot water refreshed and revived me. I only had to change into clean clothes. I thought to stay in the room and order a meal. I felt uncomfortable appearing the second day in the same dress in front of the guests. I hadn't finished my thoughts when the phone rang. It was Jan. He asked me to join them.

I went downstairs to the dining hall. We were the only guests left. Maybe because of the menace of war hanging over this once beautiful city, I struck up a carefree conversation with Jan.

"Antonija, Khalil told me that you are a good doctor. You have achieved success in healing many of the casualties of the Croatian War of Independence. Are you familiar with such cases; children like Akmed who spent their life in an atmosphere of depression, under the threat of war? I tried everything with Akmed, but he seems to be absent-minded. I am not sure how he would accept separation from his parents and if he would accept me at all as a stepfather."

"It's very hard to make progress in such cases because he is already six years old. The older the children are, the harder the separation from their parents. Although it's not always the case."

"Try to talk to him. Spend the afternoon with him. I'll go get some rest."

Akmed gladly accepted the invitation and joined me in a pleasant conversation in my hotel room. I wanted to bring him closer to the spiritual world through playfulness, feeling that this was the only path to salvation for his wounded soul. And indeed, he paid rapt attention to every word, without even being aware of it, as though he were hypnotized by it. He was repeating affirmative phrases like "being consciously aware in the present moment, opening the heart to feel the divine spark flaring within him".

Meditation was meant to clear away mental and emotional blockages caused by traumatic incidents, so he could accept reality more as it is, live in the Eternal Now and be open to giving and receiving. In order to connect him to the very Source, I needed to take him to the higher spheres of his being, so I grabbed instinctively the Shiva prayer beads and started praying for the salvation of his soul. He momentarily felt relieved after the prayer that raised a smile out of his melancholy face. Some invisible hand took the prayer beads for the nth time and started swirling them above the boy's head. I recognized Sanskrit words. They exuded the warm fragrance of sandalwood. It didn't take long to realize that it was Pandit Sati whose appearance most certainly heralded important events.

A feeling of happiness swept over me. I hugged the boy and kissed his beautiful face which lit up with joy. He responded in the same way. He took my hand and walked me to the balcony window. He pointed a finger at the open sea. The fluorescent light was barely visible in the distance. It was sparkling on the heavy sea. I remembered it from somewhere, but I didn't know from where. Its light appeared in certain intervals. The steps in the room and Khalil's voice startled me, "Unbelievable! The light is sending us a message. Kha-lil! My name! What does it all mean, Antonija?"

"The 'best friend'. Isn't that what it means in Arabic?"

THE SAME JEEP THAT was waiting for us upon our return from the mountains came to pick Jan and Akmed up. It would take them to the Refugee Reception Center and then with the first refugee convoy far beyond the borders of Lebanon.

It was hard for me to say good-bye, most of all to Akmed. His smile of happiness inspired courage in me at the moment when I lost hope in the possibility for his soul to be healed. I decided to come to grips with everything that could stand in my way, including the war. My strong desire to find Mihovil's whereabouts instinctively overpowered my desire to escape from the depressive environment. However, I was happy that at least one child was rescued. I wished the best for him and promised him that I would never stop praying for him and the good of his soul.

The hour of separation approached followed by warm kisses and the beating of hearts. I was hiding my tears. I embraced the boy firmly and grasped his hand. The driver hurried us. I had a chance to whisper to Akmed's ear, "May the Goddess Sentona be with you! May She bring you lots of happiness!"

I waved Akmed good-bye one more time. He went away in a jeep to an unknown destination, longing for a better life and hopefully leaving sorrow behind.

I wiped my tears and leaned on Khalil's shoulder. I took his arm. On the way out of the hotel, I suddenly turned to him and said, "Please, do one more thing for me. Let's go to Shatila. I want to make sure Akmed's story is true."

"To Shatila?" the waiter responded surprisingly, passing by with a drink. "I wouldn't recommend it, albeit maybe it's not too late if you want to see the real Beirut. There is some time left before the departure of the last convoy of refugees towards the Shouf mountains above Beirut."

Khalil looked at me doubtfully, then he said, "Let's go if you wish! The safest way would be to go by taxi!"

THE SHATILA REFUGEE CAMP was located about fifteen minutes from the hotel. We quickly passed through downtown and left the deserted streets. There were no passersby there or messy vegetable stallkeepers.

When we arrived at the camp, we found it to be a completely different place from the one we left behind. There were rundown caravans with dirty bazaar merchants who were selling everything from toy guns for kids to big juicy watermelons.

We were walking down the narrow streets between tall buildings. They were so close to each other that the residents were hanging their shabby clothes on a line between the buildings which blocked the sun's rays. The posters of politicians hung on worn-out walls, and there were Hezbollah flags waving on every corner of the street.

No sooner had we gotten a sense of life in the camp and wanted to get a coffee at a small improvised outdoor cafe when a street man appeared right in front of us. I could smell alcohol on his breath.

I felt startled at his appearance. I turned around to look for Khalil. I was shocked to see him running towards the stranger. The street man started punching the air with the butt of an old rifle, shouting at the top of his voice.

"Ishmael, Ishmael! God will avenge the Arabs!"

"Have you seen him?" Khalil said to him in an undertone of distrust.

The street man suddenly turned to me and said roughly, "What are you staring at? Run to the mountains, bitch!"

I grabbed my purse. I quickly put the camera into my purse and then ran towards distressed Khalil who was trying to explain something to the street man, but to no avail. He would have stayed there if a passer-by hadn't intercepted him pointing his hand towards the men in the official uniform of local police officers, most likely members of one of the militant groups. Their presence meant that it was time to go. We hurried to the hotel where the jeep was waiting for us to take us to the improvised airfield close to the Beirut Hippodrome.

We climbed into the helicopter, quickly withdrawing from the scene of war. We headed back to Keyfoun leaving behind a more or less safe place. We were moving towards uncertainty along with the thousands of refugees we could see from the air who were climbing the mountain road to the north in one of the latest convoys.

IN KEYFOUN
WITH THE
WAR REFUGEES

The convoy was slowly moving uphill. Watching from a helicopter, it looked like a snake on a serpentine trail. We suddenly lost sight of it when a big rain cloud gathered over the Keyfoun residential area as we approached the outskirts of Beirut.

Luckily we were descending as I suddenly started to feel dizzy. Khalil grabbed my hand firmly and held it until we were safely on the ground.

"Everything will be fine, Antonija," Khalil said, "when you are around me, you are safe."

I felt better as soon as we came to the village. The Sun peeked out of the horizon which eased the tension brought by the rain that had cast a shadow over the convoy of refugees.

Everything was the same as we had left it. We could hear a neighbor's dog barking, children cheering and playing as if letting us know that life in the village was still going well. Then the sound of a motor was heard and soon after an old car appeared. The perplexed faces of two little girls named Maryam and Hasna were peering out of the car. They came from southern Beirut, from the vicinity of the international airport. They were sitting shoulder to shoulder and barely said a word. They conveyed with their silence that they were taking a rest, a return to normal after the traumatic explosions caused by the Israeli attack on the nearby airport. For that reason their parents decided to send them quickly by convoy to the safety of the Beirut hills.

The girls seemed to belong to the poor members of the Muslim community. They wore torn, colorful skirts made of a cheap fabric similar to an old-fashioned cretonne. Seeing them so poorly dressed, I thought about the thousands of other children climbing the Beirut hills who left their homes either by a twist of fate or because their parents couldn't afford to feed so many children. I was wondering whether they would be taken in like little Akmed by some stranger. Or maybe I was sent to them for some reason to make their life easier.

Maryam and Hasna were the first among scores of refugees who were growing in number every day.

I started working with the children who represented the majority of the refugees. I began spending time with them day and night giving them psychological and spiritual support. My main goal was to teach them how to build Self-confidence, to increase their emotional awareness and to take responsibility for their lives. The psychotherapeutic part of the program included the teaching of conscious Self-awareness through playful experiences and imagination in order for the children to begin to heal their wounds to integrate their souls, and discover their strengths.

What I wanted the most was to imbue them with love and hope for the higher purposes of life. I encouraged them to cultivate spirituality through prayer using their own religious and spiritual traditions, to gain conscious awareness through meditation revealing more and more of their soul. This was the path of Self-healing ultimately leading to Self-realization. Bestowed by the blessings of divine power of my Goddesses of the Liburnian spiritual tradition, I tried to enliven them through visualization in order for the children themselves to receive energy and enjoy spiritual protection.

As the days passed the children were becoming more peaceful within themselves and restoring their optimism about life. The word about the woman doctor healer quickly spread. I was receiving so many refugees that I almost used up all my energy. One day Khalil recommended that I take a break and spend some time in a house in a secluded area.

THE SMALL STONE HOUSE was next to a wide trail leading deep into the forest. It was like similar traditional houses often found in Lebanon. There was, however, something odd about it – it was coalesced with rock from which a thousand year old cedar tree branched out. The master who built this beautiful house was certainly aware of its healing properties and didn't want to cut it down.

Visibly tired from my work, I flopped into something that resembled a bed. It was an improvised bed made from cedar tree branches covered with light cotton cloth with a simple, foam mattress under it.

The rest of the furniture was simple as well: a cabinet, a table, a night table and a swing chair, all made of cedar. There was another similar room to this one in the house which was Khalil's room. Next to the room were a kitchen and a bathroom with a cedar tub. There was also a generator and supplies for a month of food stored in the house.

Khalil covered me with an aromatic cedar blanket. I quickly fell asleep, stupefied by the ethereal

fragrance. I awoke early in the morning full of energy.
I washed my face in the crystal clear creek just outside the house. I felt refreshed and grabbed the Shiva
prayer beads to restore the inner beauty. Khalil was
already awake. He was sitting on a big stone behind
the tree that was standing between scattered rocks
with a steep hillside in the background. The sky above
was light azure blue with Venus floating alone in the
early morning sky.

"Then as now," Khalil turned to me, "I was gazing
at the motionless Venus light that would attract me
with its allure like a woman and draw me far away."

I was listening to Khalil and gazing at the muted
Venus light. I wanted to catch its rays and fly up
to the sky.

"Isn't it finally time to be on a first-name basis?"
Khalil interrupted my train of thought.

"Sure," I replied, surprised with his sudden inti-
macy. I also wondered if it might be time to get better
acquainted.

"Antonija, I am proud of you. You gave solace to
my suffering people. What exactly was it that attracted
them, brought them peace and gave them hope?"
Khalil raised his warm blue eyes.

"The enchantment of the Goddess. My Liburnian
Goddesses, Anzotika, Sentona, Ika, Irija were a source

of inspiration to the people from where I come from. They revealed to me a magic secret about how to open my heart, receive their energy and invoke their blessing on others."

"You are certainly bestowed with divine blessings, thanks to which you conveyed the divine energy to others and initiated healing."

"I am deeply satisfied."

"What do you feel? How have you benefited from it?"

"I feel like being touched by a higher grace that inspires me and shows me the way. I am more at peace with myself. I live a more fulfilled life, am more Self-aware, and am more conscious of others, although it means taking more responsibility."

"How do you mean?"

"I don't know. Things started changing somewhere around the last eclipse a few months ago. You probably remember it."

"Yes, it was a majestic occurrence which I'll remember for a long time."

"Then he appeared," she said, "the man whose appearance marked the beginning of a new era in my life, so to speak – a more conscious approach to life. It led me to where I am now. Although more confused, I am more conscious and more responsible for my own destiny and for the destiny of others. Mihovil was the one who enlivened my Liburnian spirit. He drew my attention to my roots and showed me how important it was to maintain a spiritual tradition. Our grandmothers were related: Mihovil said that they were keepers of an archaic tradition of mantra chanting which was passed from generation to generation from a female line. Looking for him, I have the feeling that I am reviving their eternal glory."

"Well, sometimes I have the feeling that the timeless spirit of the past reveals itself in the continuity of our actions and lives in us permanently," added Khalil. "You need to be at peace now. Relax and forget about everything for a while. Try to recall beautiful moments in your life. Come, it's an ideal place for a long walk!"

I did as Khalil told me and easily accepted his invitation. He took my hand and shouted, "Do you hear the age-old trees breathing and greeting the strangers?"

Striding on the forest path, I felt welcomed and greeted by the eternal song of the forest calling our soul to respond. I responded in the same rhythm and started singing with a clear voice. The voice filled the air reverberating through the crowns of the trees high up in the sky.

"Not so loud, Antonija! Everything is one hundred times stronger here!"

"Let it be so!" I jumped and ran into the wind that was gently pushing on the wide tree crowns.

"Just like my unlucky Hanna. Maybe you brought her back to life, and she wants to tell me through you that she is at peace."

These words made me think. It was hard to imagine how this undoubtedly beautiful woman looked. I didn't want to take her image for myself as it could lead us nowhere. I fell silent. But Khalil was in the mood to talk. He continued, "Do you know what it means to love someone who left you without telling you how much she loves you?"

"I know, Khalil. You know that I loved once and I still love. Isn't it time to forget suffering?"

"Certainly, we are not bound together by destiny in vain. I would like to sing a song for you as I used to sing for her. I am looking at you feeling her breath in your hair. I am touching her tears kissing your eyes."

"Nice. What do you want to tell me?"

"Antonija, I can't get over her. I tried to forget her by seeing the woman in you. I wanted to take you, feel you, but I couldn't."

"Let us sit down."

We had already walked far enough. I wanted to take a break. I sat right next to the trail stretching out my tired feet. I was barefoot during the whole walk without even noticing it.

Khalil sat down next to me and hugged me. His beautiful azure blue eyes reflected the sky with a small barely noticeable tear.

"My best friend, isn't it enough?"

I took Khalil's hand. I took off my Shiva prayer beads that I wore as a necklace. I wrapped them around his hand and started chanting. I started silently and then chanted louder and louder. Khalil accompanied me taking the words out of my mouth. I gave him my hands and started swirling the prayer beads above his head. I could hear the echo and then a silent sound as though it was coming out of the infinite depths of the Universe. It was getting quieter and quieter. When I was just about to get into its rhythm and penetrate deep into Self, I felt a gentle touch of the wind that brought a smell of the distant past. Then the images of the women appeared one after the other. My Goddesses were standing in front of me. Their shadows stretched slightly and I entered their energy field overwhelmed by a ray of light of a higher frequency. A sense of unity with all God's Creation permeated me. I looked at Khalil. A tear was rolling down his cheek – a tear that could have only been triggered by the power of the beauty of the Liburnian Goddess.

DEEPER INTO THE FOREST

The day passed as usual, from washing my face in the morning in a fresh creek to the short walk to a nearby forest.

Khalil and I were getting used to each other. Just when I thought things were getting better, Khalil got a phone call from his boss. He asked Khalil to come to Beirut for a few hours.

I didn't take the news well. I finally calmed down in the hope that Khalil would come back soon. The helicopter landed. We hugged each other warmly, wishing each other to enjoy the rest of the day. My heart ached as the helicopter took off high into the sky above the mountain. I thought for a moment that it was gone forever. Although it actually didn't go very far, it seemed to be going into another time. You could hear its rumbling sound echoing for a long time, overwhelming the dead silence of the surrounding nature.

I was alone. I was looking around listening

attentively to each tremble of the silent trees. I was waiting for a friendly sign from them so that I could just rush toward them and hide in their high crowns.

The shadows of the evening quietly stole upon me with their heavy rays on the threshold of the forest house. Khalil didn't come. I felt uneasy alone in the hut surrounded by the tense silence in the forest. I was lying on the bed looking into the distance while fixing my eyes upon the swinging Moon behind the window that seemed to be hanging over the nearby branches.

The hours passed by. I was trying to get to sleep by drawing the ethereal fragrance of cedar with my breath. It was tickling my nostrils making me feel more and more light-headed. In the dead of the night with my every breath, the fragrance was getting stronger and seemed to be causing at the same time a stronger rustling of the tree crowns. I was breathing, observing the rhythm of my heartbeat. I couldn't get to sleep. A disquiet was growing in me, disrupting the harmony between the supernatural atmosphere of the silent night and the idyllic beauty of Nature.

My eyes wandered for a moment behind the window, where I noticed something moving. I sat up to have better visibility. A pulsating light was glittering with the sparks of a thousand colors creating a conical beam. It was aimed toward the head of my bed. I tried to look away yet became enveloped by it. I was so completely engulfed by its glitter that it almost absorbed me. I became part of it then suddenly carried myself to some other dimension. An unpleasant, dead, cold smell permeated the air. After the light came the darkness. While I was penetrating another dimension, I could feel my soul moving. I was filled with overwhelming emotions and at times with the impulses of Self-awareness.

Hovering between the worlds embraced by the darkness, I could feel a faceless man-like being approaching. His ice cold breath was crawling over me causing an unseen fear. He had deep-set, translucent, black, hypnotic eyes. His skin was coated in gold. His dire eyes were blazing less than an inch apart when he turned to me and said in a monotone voice, "Come, sister!"

I couldn't get hold of myself as I was suddenly pulled by some force into his energetic field. I was very close to him when a voice appeared from nowhere.

"He cannot harm you!"

The being turned to me with a stern, overwhelming voice, "Look me in the eye!"

I looked at him. I found myself in his deep lamp-black eyes. They drew me in like a black hole. I was traveling through space, and then, on the other side of the black hole, I saw a barely visible figure. His outline was discernible due to a small ray of light he was spreading around himself. Some inexplicable intuition was telling me maybe it was Mihovil. I felt an arrow passing through my heart. I was motionless, feeling just a mild wince instead of the fluttering of passion that I usually felt thinking of him. I stared at the blurry figure vacantly, as though I were completely emotionless. I tried to reach him, but he avoided my gaze. After the evil being disappeared over the horizon, I heard his menacing voice, "On the Day of Judgement, you will lose all your powers!"

I flew into space holding on to the fluid cloak that appeared from somewhere around me. I was moving back and forth through time, and then suddenly everything stopped. There was nothing anymore. I fell into a deep sleep.

When I regained consciousness, I covered my face from the sun's rays that were pouring through the slightly open windows at a wide angle. Khalil was sitting next to the head of my bed.

"Khalil," I turned to him with a weak voice.

"Antonija," Khalil hugged me with paternal affection. "You don't look well. You are as white as a corpse, as though you went through the horrors of Hell."

I hardly sat up, squaring my elbows. I took a short

breath and then said in a harsh tone, "How could you have left me alone in this forest house?"

"I was only supposed to leave for a few hours. I have spent countless nights here alone."

"I don't know why I even accepted the invitation."

"We won't get anywhere blaming each other. Tell me finally what happened," Khalil said raising his voice.

"If I could only remember. I was waiting for you to come back. I couldn't sleep and then I suddenly fell asleep and must have had a nightmare. I am exhausted. My mind is blank as though my memory was erased."

"You will get better in time. You have to rest," Khalil said warmly, "now, I would like to tell you some news that you would like to know. Your mysterious friend most likely left Lebanon. My friends from the police told me."

I had a vague foreboding of something sad that could happen to Mihovil. It crossed my mind that Khalil must have had good relationships with the police being so well informed. I could hardly follow him. I was drifting off into sleep as my heavy eyelids finally closed. I was listening to Khalil half-asleep.

"Mihovil must have left something. Do you remember something typical of him, something that he said?"

Visualizing Mihovil's image, a thought suddenly

came to me and I whispered it in Khalil's ear, kissing him gently, "Clear the name of the ancient Liburnians!" These were the last words that I could remember Mihovil saying.

JERUSALEM PROPHET

III

FAREWELL TO KHALIL

After the Lebanese-Israeli conflict ended, people swarmed the streets of Beirut again. Only a few people among the crowd who had worried looks on their faces would remind you that the ghost of war was still hovering over the city. As life began returning to normal, I started feeling better.

Khalil invited me one Sunday to his house. It was the first time that he had invited me to his Beirut home. I felt welcomed at once in such a relaxed atmosphere accentuated by the color of lavender on the walls.

I dropped my belongings and then went out to the terrace where Khalil was already drinking his morning coffee. It was still warm, although signs of autumn were beginning to appear. You could feel a gentle touch of a shifting wind that was blowing in from the sea bringing fresh air.

"Have a seat!" Khalil turned to me.

"Nice place you have here. Your house is like

the residence of a president." I couldn't escape the impression it made on me.

"It's my father's inheritance," Khalil said briefly and continued cheerfully, "I hope you have had some rest."

"Yes I have, although I haven't calmed down completely."

"I know what bothers you. You surely would like to know if there is any news about Mihovil."

My lips quivered with a smile just remembering Mihovil. I pricked up my ears anticipating what Khalil would tell me.

"Antonija, we are on his trail. American social worker Jan from Shatila was right. He was last seen in Jerusalem."

"In Jerusalem?" I gave an exclamation.

"Would you like to go to Israel?" Khalil looked at me questioningly.

"To Israel?"

"Don't you want to look for Mihovil?"

"I have wanted nothing else since the beginning," I said involuntarily. I continued doubtfully, "I have spent the whole summer in Lebanon. I should be back in Croatia. I don't know what my Professor will say to that."

"Everything has been taken care of," Khalil said persuasively.

"I don't understand. Have you talked to him?"

"Dr. Fathima has intervened. Dr. Sandalic has helped. Your Professor has granted you a sabbatical year until next autumn. He agreed to take your lectures."

"Who will finance my stay?"

"You are going to the Hadassah Mt. Scopus University Hospital, well-known for its medical center and excellent school of public health. Your stay will be financed by the Israeli government."

"That's amazing! Not many people have the opportunity to be a part of their team of well-recognized experts."

"You will be satisfied."

"That's wonderful," I said being caught unaware by such an outcome including surprise at Khalil's high position and influence.

"Antonija," he said after a short pause, "take this note and remember the phone number. It's the number of Jerusalem's Rabbi Yitzhak. He will give you shelter if you need it. Call him only in an emergency."

"That's fine; I understand."

Khalil gently kissed me on my forehead and

said, "You are leaving tomorrow. It's your day today, Antonija. What would be your wish?"

"Just stay with me and keep me company. Who knows when we shall meet again. Let's enjoy the sun and talk."

We stayed on the terrace until the evening. We would have spent the night there if Khalil's cook hadn't called us to a delicious dinner that I would remember for a long time. I was most impressed by his art of mixing spices that would improve the taste of every Arab dish. As a vegetarian, I was served with the traditional Arabic salad Tabouli[47]. Mint, cinnamon and nutmeg gave this dish an exotic taste. What was most interesting was that the ingredients were wrapped in lettuce leaves and eaten with the hands.

Khalil and I said our friendly good-byes to each other with an understanding look in our eyes trying to avoid emotions. Before joining the other passengers and leaving for Israel, Khalil threw me a kiss. He shouted to me, "I am with you! Khalil, your best friend!"

---

[47] Taboûleh, Ar. – salad made of bulgur wheat, parsley, mint, tomato, lemon, cabbage and seasonings according to taste.

ON THE WAY TO JERUSALEM

The flight to Tel Aviv was fairly monotonous until we landed in Amman, at which point a Jordanian physician, Abdulah, joined me. He was a short man in his thirties; chatty and well-mannered, quite different from my perception of intrusive Arab men.

I learned a lot from Abdulah's story about the Jersualem's Hadassah Hospital[48]. He went there to take his final specialization examination in reconstructive surgery. He was employed at the Amman's Red Crescent[49] Hospital and was working together with the physicians from the medical, humanitarian organization Doctors Without Borders on a reconstructive surgery program for treating casualties of the Iraqi war.

I knew that Hadassah Medical Center treated

---

[48] Haddassah University Hospital opened in 1939 on Mount Scopus in Jerusalem.

[49] Jordan Red Crescent Hospital is a non-profit hospital, established in 1948.

casualties from both sides of the front line, Israelis as well as Palestinians. And yet I didn't know that it excelled in promoting peace and was nominated for the Nobel Peace Prize. Perhaps this is the reason why Abdulah was well accepted, like many other Arabs and Palestinians from many areas on the West Bank who would return there after their specialization. By the way, I had the opportunity to witness it myself, working with different nationalities. Maybe it was one of the unique places on Earth where minorities as well as foreigners were in leading positions. I took a job as the head of the very busy Outpatient Posttraumatic Stress Disorder Department where patients might have been waiting for months to get medical care.

I forgot myself while talking to Abdulah so that I barely noticed we were approaching Ben Gurion International Airport in Tel Aviv. Feeling a little dizzy when the plane started making a hasty landing, I took Abdulah's hand and raised my finger signaling him to be quiet, which he did immediately. He broke the silence when the plane landed and the happy passengers erupted in applause. Soon a commotion started. I didn't have time to say good-bye to Abdulah. When we were approaching passport control, I just nodded to him in greeting. Abdulah went to his passport control line and proceeded to a special processing area. I went towards my passport control line getting rid of a chatty, travel mate.

Arriving at the Tel Aviv Airport, I immediately went to the taxi stand. I was welcomed warmly again thanks to my friendship with Khalil. His longtime friend Ibrahim, a Palestinian from Eastern Jerusalem was waiting for me. His rough features made him appear to be a farm laborer rather than a bard with a refined, high level sensitivity towards music interpretation. All the way to Jerusalem he was singing the songs from his repertoire and I arrived refreshed to Jerusalem. Enchanted by his singing, I didn't pay attention to the road as I normally enjoy doing when I arrive at a new tourist destination.

All the way to Jerusalem I delighted in Ibrahim's high pitched voice. He reminded me of our folk singers except that his singing was indeed artistic.

Ibrahim accompanied me to the hotel lobby. I promised to call him as soon as I acclimatized myself. I was sure that he would be a good guide and felt intuitively that he would be a solid support in the days ahead.

FIRST IMPRESSIONS
OF JERUSALEM

I settled into the Ambassador Hotel, one of the decent hotels in Jerusalem where affluent and medium-income guests like to stay. It was located in the residential, consular district Sheikh Jarrah[50] at a short distance from Mount Scopus, on a hill that offered a splendid view of Jerusalem.

By choosing a hotel with a tastefully decorated room, piquant dishes, and always smiling personnel, including the owner of the hotel Sami Abudaya, who personally welcomed the guests, Khalil seemed to know my taste. I was surprised that the hotel was situated in Eastern Jerusalem, the predominantly Arab part of the city. The guests were mixed, from Palestinians and Arabs to European dignitaries. I came across a few guests from Israel, usually Israeli scientists who were frequent symposium attendees.

---

[50] A Palestinian neighborhood in East Jerusalem on the slopes of Mount Scopus north of the Old City.

After I settled into my room, Dr. David came to
see me. He was one of the four from our group with
whom I would spend most of the next year at the
Outpatient Posttraumatic Stress Disorder Department
of Jerusalem's Hadassah Hospital.

David was a Jew from West Jerusalem. He was of
medium build and a bit stocky. He wore a sport T-shirt,
jeans and Jesus sandals. Seeing him so dressed, I
immediately felt a closeness which I often feel with
people radiating simplicity and depth of vision. David
had a Jewish skullcap that covered the little hair that
he had left.

David came to see me when I was unpacking my
baggage in my room. He invited me to dinner at the
restaurant Culinaria, one of the most popular restaurants on the famous street Cardo[51] in the Jewish district, just a few minutes away from the hotel.

Walking through the Old City, I was enjoying rem-
nants of the past and carefully listening to David. He
talked at tedious length about the hospital and the
high professionalism of his colleagues at work. I would
have been happier if he had told me more about this
part of the city. Instead, I only saw the picturesque
street Cardo with a lot of small shops that were selling

[51] The Cardo was the main street in Ancient Roman Cities. It is
the part of the Old City's Jewish Quarter in Jerusalem.

everything – from women's scarves to rose and olive wood rosaries. When we were within reach of the restaurant Culinaria, a brightly lit small shop drew my attention. I noticed a mirror close to the front door. It reflected the image of an old Jew with a long beard and notably wilted cheeks. He was looking at me, or so it seemed to me. I wanted to go in, but David pulled me on my sleeve telling me that we were almost at the restaurant and we could come back later.

The first moment I entered the restaurant Culinaria, it gave me the feeling of being in the Roman Empire that I had felt while walking on the streets and peering into the houses and ancient shrines. As we walked through the Roman atmosphere and decor of the restaurant, the waiters in togas welcomed us, gave us togas and bay-wreaths, and accompanied us to a private dining-room.

After drinks, we were offered something like Middle Eastern bread with olive oil and a mixture of spices. We continued eating the light buffet with side dishes of zucchini, fresh dill, lettuce and mushrooms. They served a juicy watermelon as a dessert, rarely seen on restaurant menus.

David impressed me with his eloquence and knowledge of medicine. I thought he would tell me more about the history of this part of the world, but he got so engrossed in other conversation topics that there was no time for that. However, I didn't regret not having a better guide as it was getting late and I wanted to get some rest.

THE HADASSAH HOSPITAL

The Hadassah Hospital made a good impression on me, unlike similar large medical complexes.

My department and study room were located on the back side of the building, high on a hill. The low window had visibility of a wide plot of mown grass surrounded by small pine trees and a big cactus leaning towards the window.

The hospital staff were nice and responsive. David, under whose supervision I started working, told me rule number one which was that there was equality, regardless of race, gender and religion. Maybe this was the reason that, from the very first day, I felt relaxed in our small team of four physicians. Besides David, there was Abdul from nearby Bethlehem[52] and Maha from the Muslim Quarter of the Old City of Jerusalem.

My colleagues were very simple: Abdul wore work

---

[52] The Biblical birthplace of Jesus. A Palestinian town south of Jerusalem in the West Bank.

clothes without any special distinguishing religious marks and Maha, a Muslim woman, had a beige scarf wrapped around her head and neck. She shook my hand right away and smiled at me which told me that I could rely on her and wouldn't have any problems as women sometimes have with each other.

David was the only one who seemed to have a philosophically oriented mind. I didn't mind as I could carry on discussions with him about anything, even about topics typically not wise to talk about with staff. I could talk to David about world politics, climate change, Jews and Muslims and, strangely enough, about Armageddon. He brought it up in the early days of our friendship and reminded me of the events I had already put behind me.

We started talking accidentally about Armageddon during our regular lunch break. Abdul and Maha were with us, and David was hesitant in their presence. He changed the subject rapidly, which surprised me. I thought maybe he didn't want to bore these two uninformed physicians, such as they seemed to me, with such stories. I soon forgot all of that until David and I met one day next to the hospital windows painted by Marc Chagall[53] himself. According to David, it was the ideal place for such secret conversations.

[53] Marc Chagall (1887-1985) – French painter born to a Jewish

"Antonija," David turned to me, "it's one thing that the story about Armageddon may seem to be insignificant to the uninformed, but another thing is how he may perceive it. After all, it's about the war. Be careful. There are informers."

David's serious look left me speechless. I gulped audibly, thinking how not even here in Israel, far away, would I have peace. David's friendly tone of voice calmed me down.

"Let's have a coffee."

We went downstairs towards the nearby coffee bar in the hospital complex. We ordered two ice teas and a double coffee.

David's invitation was a friendly gesture and, regardless of his comment, I started thinking of him as a friend. Although we were close in age, he was like a father to me, a protector and counselor, who would sometimes tell me off when necessary. However, first and foremost he was a friend who gave me professional and moral support which was so important to me, being so far away from home.

David stood up and put the tray down. He looked into my eyes and said, "Try not to be seen much with

family in Vitebsk, then in the Russian Empire, today in Belarus. He had significant influence on modern art. He synthesized Jewish spirituality with Russian folk tradition and French Modernism.

me. Get closer to Maha. She is a good person. You will be happier in a woman's company."

I AGREED TO GET to know this modest woman of a gentle disposition. When David approached her, she was happy about taking me to the Jerusalem market in the Old City, called Shuk[54] in Hebrew.

I was very delighted to accept her invitation knowing that this was the best way to become friends and to find out more about this wonderful woman. We went to the market on my first day off on Saturday after my first two weeks in Jerusalem.

It was a bright day that was enough to lift my spirits. I was in an even better mood when we arrived at the market and I saw stalls with displays of abundant goods under colorful umbrellas next to the tall walls. There were spices of all sorts, candies, fruits and vegetables, souvenirs, pottery, oriental clothes and jewelry.

Like most women, the stall with clothes attracted my attention the most. I spent most of my time there, picking through the garments. I liked to touch them, feeling their texture with my fingers to determine their quality. I held a silk garment in my hand while

---

[54] The Jerusalem Shuk market is the largest market in Jerusalem and one of the most famous in the Middle East.

talking to a street vendor. Maha was translating. She was bargaining with the vendor and I was looking at colorful silver, gold, and red-embroidered tunics. I unfolded one of them and to my astonishment I saw behind the stall a familiar face. It was Ibrahim, Khalil's friend who waited for me at the airport. He smiled at me revealing one golden tooth in the upper front. Watching him I noticed a light scar on his forehead that I didn't notice at our first meeting.

Ibrahim was looking at me with slightly sad, drowsy, green eyes that appeared accentuated because of his tanned, wrinkled skin. He greeted me, warmly shaking my hand. He greeted Maha briefly, excusing himself for being busy. It was one of those days when you meet someone you least expect to see, yet someone who gives you a smile that can make your day.

I felt comfortable in Maha's company, most of all because she was calm and reserved. She was the type of person who inspired confidence, someone to whom you can open your heart. I didn't want to intrude. I approached her and asked if she was single or if there was someone. She said she had someone, but nothing serious. She asked me if I had someone and I said that maybe fate brought me here to look for him. Then Maha smiled saying that hopefully I would have luck.

We left the stalls with clothes and souvenirs.

Talking as friends, we walked further on the famous King David Street in the Old City with many shops and art galleries. We went into one gallery where a beautiful picture with the two, bluish horses on a white background by Israeli painter Reuven Rubin[55] attracted my attention. There was an Arab in white clothes with a white headband and a sword in his hand riding one of the horses. His face amazingly resembled Mihovil's, bringing me back to the reality of Jerusalem.

As chance would have it, we separated at the Jaffa Gate[56] where to my astonishment we saw an entertainer with a snake. It was wrapped around his neck. He almost lost it while we were passing by. It was an omen that confirmed my belief of a snake playing a special role in my destiny.

---

[55] Reuven Rubin (1893-1974) – Israeli painter of Romanian origin who integrated the elements of Naïve and Impressionist art.

[56] Jaffa Gate is a 16th century gate, one of the seven, main, open gates in Jerusalem's Old City Walls.

THE GYPSY WOMAN'S PROPHECY

T he day began as usual but without Abdul. He came a little bit later. We were taking turns to reduce stress and make our work easier.

By noon, the waiting room was empty. While Maha, David, and I were talking during the lunch break, Abdul showed up at my office's door.

"Does anyone have any headache medication? It is nearly impossible for me to endure it!" he said openly which was unusual for this private, odd, and a bit cold man.

"Here you are," I passed a medication to Abdul.

"What happened?" David asked him.

"I spent all morning at a psychiatric facility. Do you remember the Gypsy woman who used to come to tell us our fortune?"

"Of course," Maha replied.

"I finally hospitalized her. The hospital is reluctant to admit outpatients, but the woman became completely dissociative, foretelling the end of the world, so they had to admit her. I came to ask for help, David. Can you persuade the Head of the Psychiatric Department to keep her?"

"Sure."

"I'll go with you," Maha said.

Abdul and I were left alone. After a moment of silence, we exchanged glances, looking each other up and down.

"How are you doing, Antonija? Have you gotten used to us and Jerusalem?" Abdul said.

"Thank you for asking. You are great company and an expert in many things. It's my honor to work with you. And it's not hard to get accustomed to Jerusalem. I am not sure if I saw a more beautiful city except maybe Beirut."

I paused while mentioning Beirut, thinking that it would be better not to mention awful events that happened not long ago. But to my astonishment, Abdul, usually not talkative and focused on his work, showed much interest in them. He was deeply impressed by my work with the refugees in the Shouf Mountains above Beirut. It was, of course, only what I told him about my activity in Lebanon. He was asking with curiosity mostly about my healing abilities. I thought it was just a professional curiosity.

David and Maha showed up at the door and interrupted our conversation. They conveyed the latest news about the bomb attack that happened recently close to the Tower of David[57]. This meant we had to work more hours tonight and wait to admit casualties, some of whom might need psychological help. My colleagues were ready to act immediately after hearing the news. They grabbed their working clothes and we went together towards the ambulance.

I was the last one to get there. I attended the last casualty who was brought from the scene of the accident. Coincidence or not, as fate would have it the Jewish student Abraham was shot by a bullet fired by a Palestinian from Eastern Beirut in the vicinity of the Tower of David, the symbol of Jerusalem.

In the panic not to lose the young man's life, I ran after the cart with his massacred body. Abdul came running to help holding the oxygen mask so that it would not fall off the patient's face. Although he wasn't our patient, we had to be ethical and accompany each of the heavily injured who were taken into surgery.

The surgery lasted twelve hours. Both legs of the young man were amputated. With such difficult cases, I would usually wait around until the end of the

---

[57] The Tower of David is the medieval citadel located near the Jaffa Gate.

surgery. This time, since it was a complicated surgery, I took turns with Abdul and Maha. Not only his physical body, but his mental condition was dependent on the outcome of the surgery.

That night around dawn after I managed to get some sleep, I returned to the operating room entrance hall where I left my glasses. As I entered the hall I heard voices coming from the operating room. I could recognize men's voices but I wasn't sure who was talking. As I came closer to the entrance door I could hear them, "The Gypsy woman wasn't far from the truth. Soon, in the most holy site…" Then I heard footsteps, and the door opened slightly. I quickly grabbed my glasses and ran away.

IN THE HOLY SITES
OF JERUSALEM

I spent a week sitting next to the young man's bed whose limbs were torn apart. I gave up any hope that he would regain consciousness. Yet, on Friday, when I was about to go home, the young man opened his deep, sad, brown eyes that only a few days ago were radiating joy. I held his hand. He responded with a handshake. His beautiful, starry eyes peering out of the thick bandage gripped my heart.

"Everything will be all right. Don't worry," he said softly after I gave an exclamation of relief.

"You can freely leave him to me," a doctor on duty said. "Go home, Antonija."

"I'll pray for him. That is the only wise thing I can do for him," I said.

The young man's condition inspired me to take the path from the Mount of Olives along the Via Dolorosa[58],

---

[58] Via Dolorosa or the "Way of Sorrows" is believed to be the path that Jesus walked on the way to his crucifixion.

the "Way of Sorrows" to the Old City. That walk was a great joy for every Christian. I wasn't a practicing Christian, yet I felt that in this case I should lay aside the Shiva prayer beads and do something from the tradition I was born in. I thought maybe it would be a good idea to have a guide, so I decided to call Ibrahim and ask him to go with me. He wasn't home in the evening when I called. I left a message and went to bed. I didn't have to wait long. He called me in the morning to tell me that he had been expecting my call for a long time and that he would be with me in a minute.

It was late in the morning when Ibrahim arrived. He was chatty and cheerful. His face broke into a wide smile on seeing me.

"How are you doing, Antonija? Would you like to have company on today's excursion?"

"Certainly," I answered while shaking his hand.

Ibrahim shook my hand and kissed me on my forehead. Seeing him so carefree and light-hearted, I cheered up as well, forgetting for a moment the bad events.

"Well, which way would you like to take?" he asked me.

"The one which any sincere Christian would take, to the Mount of Olives[59], of course."

---

[59] The Mount of Olives was the Eastern border of Ancient

The Sun was high in the sky and its warm rays shining down on us was such a comfort to me. It was late autumn, almost winter. However, the weather was still nice enough for us to go on foot. It didn't seem far, even though we were walking at a slow pace to the Mount of Olives.

Ibrahim was silent the whole way, not wanting to interrupt my thoughts. My countenance conveyed a pensive and absent disposition. He finally spoke when we arrived at the foothills of the Mount of Olives. He asked me if there was anything else I would like to see. I said I would like to stop for a while at the Gethsemane Garden[60] and pray at the place where Jesus prayed for the last time.

When I came to the garden, I stood under the first olive tree. As soon as I grabbed its soft twig, it seemed to me that I awakened Jesus's eternal energy, feeling a higher holy power pouring into me. I burst into tears out of rapture. Ibrahim turned to me.

"Is everything all right, Antonija?" Seeing the expression on my face – an inner glowing ardor – he realized that I was in a state of a special spiritual ecstasy, so he offered to take me to the nearby Tomb

Jerusalem and the location of many Biblical events.

[60] The Gethsemane Garden at the foot of the Mount of Olives is a place where Jesus prayed on the night of his betrayal and arrest. It is named in the New Testament (Mark 14:32-50).

of the Virgin Mary[61]. This place was also a holy site to Muslims because Muhammad saw a light over the tomb during his Night Journey from Mecca to Jerusalem. As my attention shifted, I said that I would be glad to go.

A small Orthodox Church was located at the place of the Tomb of the Virgin Mary. Seeing it was really inspiring. The icons of the church created a distinctive artistic ambience with an ancient ambience created by its hanging lamps. I tried to imagine the light that Muhammad saw, and I finally calmed down.

On the way back to Jerusalem, we went through the Lions' Gate[62], and then continued walking the Via Dolorosa, the Stations of the Cross. We stopped in front of the Mosque of Omar[63]. I recognized its tall glittering dome that I had seen from a distance on our walk from the Mount of Olives. When I came to the front of the mosque, I gave an exclamation upon hearing Ibrahim's words.

"Here we are, in the most holy site of Jerusalem," he said in a solemn voice.

---

[61] The Tomb of the Virgin Mary at the foot of Mount of Olives is believed by Eastern Christians to be the burial place of Mary, the mother of Jesus.

[62] The Lions' Gate is an easterly gate of Jerusalem's Old City. Its name comes from the pairs of stone lions seen on either side of the entrance.

[63] The Mosque of Omar is the place where the great caliph Omar conquered Jerusalem in 638 A.D.

"In the most holy site of Jerusalem?"

"What's going on, Antonija? What are you confused about?"

"Isn't it the Church of the Holy Sepulchre[64]?"

"Yes, for Christians. But for the Jews, it's the Mount of Moriah[65], today the site of the Mosque of Omar where God promised to Abraham and his descendants the land of Israel. According to Jewish belief it is the location from where the world expanded into its present form and where God gathered the dust used to create the first man, Adam. For us Muslims, it's the holy site from where Muhammad ascended into heaven. It's the root of trouble that can lead to bloodshed because the Jews want to destroy the mosque and build a Jewish temple there."

"Ibrahim, then this place is ... "

I didn't finish my thought as Ibrahim interrupted me when we saw the Orthodox believers walking in the procession with the tall crucifix carried at the head of the procession. I fixed my eyes on one of the priests in a long black robe and a gray beard. Then it seemed to

---

[64] The Church of the Holy Sepulchre is the place where Jesus is said to have been buried. Several denominations share this site today, mainly the Greek Orthodox Church and the Armenian Orthodox Church.

[65] The Mount of Moriah is the location of the sacrifice of Abraham's son Isaac. (Genesis 22:2).

me that I saw David about a hundred meters behind him chasing after someone in a leather coat and sunglasses, who looked like a man from another world.

"Ibrahim, look!" I pulled him on his sleeve.

"Let's go!" He quickly took my hand and began running.

We briefly stopped at the "Wailing Wall"[66], then continued running the remaining long distance. I thought that I saw David again passing by a bit farther. He threw Ibrahim a glance heading in the direction of the Jewish Quarter.

"What does it all mean?" I asked Ibrahim nervously.

"I'll explain later. David is our man," he managed to say. "Let's go back to Via Dolorosa!"

"I would like to see the Church of the Holy Sepulchre."

"Look, we are almost there," Ibrahim added.

Soon we were in the Church of the Holy Sepulchre, at the last station of the Cross. We went towards the site where Jesus is traditionally believed to be crucified. We were standing under the open dome looking into a spot in the sky from where a bright sunray was

---

[66] The Western or Wailing Wall is an ancient limestone wall in the Old City of Jerusalem. It is a place of prayer and pilgrimage, sacred to the Jewish people, where they came to mourn the ruin of the Temple destroyed by the Romans in 70 A.D.

radiating. The sunray appeared light blue in color. The light spreading through the whole church made for a miraculous, mystical atmosphere. Ibrahim said that the mysterious light appears every year on Great Saturday reviving the atmosphere of the crucifixion for the Christians.

Under the spell of the splendid atmosphere and the mystical light over the church candles and oil lamps, I managed to push to the back of my mind the dreaded thought that maybe the Mount of Moriah was the holy site where the prophecy of the Gipsy woman would be fulfilled. I said good-bye to Ibrahim and hurried towards the New Gate[67], the exit of the Old City.

---

[67] The New Gate on the west side of the Old City walls wasn't part of the original design of the 16th century walls. It was built in 1889.

AT THE DEAD SEA

I had been expecting something to happen for a week and was relieved when Ibrahim came on Friday, cheerful as usual, with the news that he was taking me to the Dead Sea[68].

The weather was still warm. The closer we got to the desert, the more the roaring, east wind Hamsin was blowing and raising the desert sand. It was maybe the last heat wave before the upcoming rainfall which meant that we could take a swim in the sea.

We were driving in the West Bank where it was safe to drive according to the Tourist Office. We arrived at the Dead Sea in less than an hour. The road was well below sea level. We continued towards the south to Ein Gedi[69], an oasis along the coast of the Dead Sea. Tourists came there from all over the world to enjoy a desert adventure.

---

[68] The Dead Sea is the lowest place on Earth (431 meters below sea level). Its water is unusually salty. It is bordered by Jordan to the East and Israel and the West Bank to the West.

[69] Ein Gedi in Israel is an oasis and the nature reserve.

Finding myself at the lowest place on Earth, four hundred meters below sea level, was really an adventure. I felt our visit to Israel wouldn't have been complete without seeing this oasis. It was a wonderful, almost idyllic place adorned by lush vegetation, with a stunning view of the cliffs on the Jordanian side of the coast.

We settled into separate rooms at the Kibbutz[70] Hotel. We were tired and went to bed early. After breakfast, we went to the sea. I was so delighted to go into the sea, however, because of the high salt concentration, I could only float, not really swim.

We spent the morning floating in the sea, enjoying the healing sea water. Ibrahim chose the water for a private conversation. So, while the others were reading books, we wore straw hats and began a conversation about the end of the world prophesied by the eccentric Gypsy woman. Ibrahim, to my astonishment, was very talkative and I was glad to share my thoughts with him about this mysterious subject.

"Antonija, Khalil sends you his regards."

I was wondering how much Ibrahim knew about everything that had happened in the last few months

---

[70] Kibbutz is a collective traditionally community, farm-based, in Israel. The first kibbutz was established in 1909.

and how much I could trust him. I was relieved when he started talking and realized that I was in good hands and I could trust Ibrahim completely.

"Antonija, I don't know how much you know about the events of the last week. Although they don't seem to be linked, there is a strange coincidence between our seeing our colleague David in front of the Mosque of Omar and your hearing the Gypsy woman's prophecy."

"Do you know David?"

"Yes, we both work for the Israeli Secret Service."

"Secret Service?" I uttered with bated breath.

"I thought you knew it from Khalil," Ibrahim looked at me questioningly.

I pulled myself together keeping a straight face and I crossed my arms and continued calmly, "How long have you been in touch with Khalil?"

"Since a young man named Ishmael appeared at the Shatila Palestinian refugee camp in Beirut," Ibrahim said confidently.

"Humph," I paused and then asked, "what have you found out?"

"We are doing everything possible so that things don't get out of hand," Ibrahim said taking my hand, "Antonija, you can trust me."

"I know," I said while playing the events in my head as the pieces of the puzzle were falling into place. Khalil a secret agent? His secrecy turned out to be legitimate. He was a great actor. It all fit into the larger picture: the acute intuitiveness of an investigator, his ease of movement in dangerous places, his ability to be at my disposal when necessary, and his minimizing of danger, like when my hotel room in Beirut was searched. Above all, he was well-informed about Mihovil's whereabouts.

It was hard for me to associate Mihovil with the image of Ishmael in the photo in the school newspaper of the United Nations-run school at the Shatila Palestinian refugee camp: a bearded Arab man in a long white dress with a cloth wrapped around his neck and one arm, and his name tattooed on the other arm. I wasn't quite clear why every time I thought of him, I imagined a strange figure, a being with deep-set, translucent, black, hypnotic eyes and skin coated in gold. Something told me that he contained the clue to the mysterious double of Ishmael and Mihovil. Then the image of a hut in the Beirut hills flashed upon me. A vague figure appeared to me and I felt thrilled in its presence. The apparition didn't last long. I couldn't remember anything anymore. I had black spots before

my eyes, and then there was darkness. I could only
hear Ibrahim's voice, "I have confidence in David as a
skillful agent. He will catch the young man, whether
he is a prophet or a petty crook."

I was relieved, realizing that Ibrahim didn't associate Ishmael with Mihovil. However, I was confused
thinking of David running after someone a few days
ago when Ibrahim and I saw him in front of the
Mosque of Omar. But I didn't want to go into detail,
I let Ibrahim talk. I caught his last words and was
startled when I heard him discussing an informer, "I
would like to add to what you heard at the hospital:
Your superior, Dr. Benjamin told me in confidence
about an informer in the hospital."

"I know, David already warned me. Is Dr. Benjamin
with you as well?"

"Yes, he is the head of the intelligence wing of the
Israeli Police Department at Hadassah Hospital. He
thinks that an informer is in touch with the person
who, God forbid, would cause a grievous incident on
a big religious holiday."

Oh my God! I murmured to myself. "Do you know
if he suspects someone?"

"No, although he thinks it may be one of the
physicians."

"In the department?"

"I don't know. He thinks it could be any one of the physicians. You can help us with this, Antonija."

"When do you expect it to happen?"

"Soon. There is something else. I have a feeling it wouldn't be the main event. It will precede something even bigger. We have to stop the person who would take part in it."

After the conversation with Ibrahim, I didn't feel like swimming anymore. The blue sky was overcast with dark clouds announcing the rain.

The rest of the day I spent in the hotel room thinking about everything I had heard. A sense of foreboding came over me. Even Ibrahim couldn't drive the feeling away during the pleasant dinner. I managed to dispel it late in the evening when I came to my room. I went to the balcony to close the door. I opened the curtains and gazed towards the restless, sparkling, foamy waves in the distance. I saw a fluorescent light on the opposite side of the coast with dark clouds hovering over it. It seemed to float at a constant height above the surface. I was fascinated by its supernatural glow. I wasn't surprised as I felt for a moment a Divine Presence. I wanted Ibrahim to see it, and he, as though knowing it, joined me on the balcony of the adjoining room.

"Everything will be all right, Antonija! 'We are with you', this message says." Ibrahim took a break and continued, "And I am with you, and I'll protect you, and I'll give my life for you, if necessary."

SHAMIL

This morning the city was awakening to dense hazy ominous-looking clouds looming over it.

I went to work on foot. After about half an hour, I heard a taxi siren wailing behind me. The taxi driver stopped the car and turned to me astonished in broken English, "Mam, hurry up before the rain comes."

I managed to get to the department before the rain started pouring down and the flood swept everything away. On the way to my room, the electricity went out. I stopped for a moment and then went into the room. I heard strong thunder. The walls started shaking and the hanging lamp started swaying. I lost my balance and fell on the chair. I was close to the window when I heard a barely audible sound outside. I had the feeling that someone was sneaking around the cactus by my window. I didn't understand how anyone happened to be outside and survive the lightning strike right behind my window. Unless it was someone or something with supernatural power that wanted to let me know that it was waiting for me. I was startled by my realization. Then the generator started working and the phone rang instantly. It was Dr. Benjamin. He asked me to come to him.

We were the only ones in the department. The building felt oddly empty. The silence between the claps of thunder created an atmosphere of unearthly void.

I entered Dr. Benjamin's room. Seeing me so beside myself, he hugged me like a father. He caressed my hair and said, "Have a seat, Antonija. What happened?"

"Dr. Benjamin, I think that someone was following me outside."

"Who would be outside now? Calm down. There is nothing to fear. Whoever gets in your way won't harm you."

Then the door opened. Abdul showed up wet to the skin. He was staring at us with a horrified look as though he just tore himself away from the hug of a monster.

"I was looking for you in your room," he said shivering from the cold.

"What happened, Abdul?"

"The storm caught me on the way from the parking lot. I came from the back. The sky was suddenly lit up with a powerful strike of lightning followed by a frightening clap of thunder. I fell to the ground and then ran into the nearby bushes."

"What were you doing in the bushes?"

"I was waiting for the thunder and lightning to stop."

"Waiting for them to stop? Why did you come? You should have stayed home."

"I wanted to help. There is a lot of work to do with the medical records."

"Here, you can have these scrubs. Get changed," Dr. Benjamin gave him the medical scrubs.

Abdul thanked him, then went to change clothes behind the partition. When he came back, he grabbed the medical records folder and went towards his room.

Dr. Benjamin and I exchanged glances. I stood up without saying a word and took my medical records folder.

"Take Maha's as well," Dr. Benjamin said after a short break.

"I cannot. These are not the medical records of my patients," I said in astonishment.

"Don't worry, Maha won't mind. We have to submit a medical bulletin tomorrow. Pay attention to the psychological, personality profile of the difficult patients."

I went towards my room, but I stopped at Maha's room. I opened her cabinet drawer and took the folder.

Then I heard a noise. I continued. I was safe behind the hermetically sealed windows through which no one would try to enter during such bad weather. I turned the light on. I was leafing through the documents with nothing special in mind. When I was almost done and wanted to put them aside, one of our many patients with multiple personality disorders caught my eye. It was a man named Shamil. He was a middle-aged, family man who made a career as a business consultant at a large commercial company. He felt he had a powerful mind. Maha's remarks in the margins drew my attention: *soulbound* rather than classical multiple personality disorder. In modern terminology, *soulbound* is related to people who assume the role of a particular fictional character.

Shamil took on the identity of a being with supernatural power. That was unusual. I read further that Shamil was abused as a child which could account for his classical multiple personality disorder and his posttraumatic stress. *Soulbound* personalities often took on fictitious identities of historical figures, movie or book characters, or people they were in previous lives or even future. In Shamil's case, it was *superman*. Maha for some reason left a blank space under the section "more detailed description of personality".

I put the pen aside and then finished writing:

"finalize the details." I felt quite uncomfortable looking through a colleague's folders with classified information about her patients. I was, however, interested in the case. I wanted to discuss it with Maha at any rate. I was curious about her schedule. I moved her desk calendar closer so I could read it. I couldn't believe my eyes when I read: "Shamil, Monday at eleven". I looked at the antique clock in Maha's office and saw that it was almost eleven o'clock. I was surprised to see a cuckoo in the upper window of the clock ready to appear when the clock struck the hour.

I laid the documents aside. I went towards the door to turn the light off when the cuckoo chimed eleven. I quickly opened the door and backed away. Maha was standing at the door wet to the skin, stained with mud and weeping.

"Good gracious, what happened?" I yelled.

I grabbed a towel to wrap it around Maha's body when I saw her hair full of grass and cactus needles. "Shamil," I uttered a scream. "Hurry up, we need to get to Dr. Benjamin."

We rushed along the corridor and climbed up the stairs to the raised ground floor. I felt relieved when I saw Dr. Benjamin in his room. He was sitting with his glasses on, reading Abdul's remarks on patients' charts.

"Abdul already turned in his report," Dr. Benjamin said to me. "What happened to you?" he exclaimed, turning toward Maha.

"He ambushed me... "

"And almost killed her!" I said to Dr. Benjamin with a raised voice.

"I assumed," he responded calmly and then hugged Maha. "I know about your relationship. You initiated a romantic relationship with a patient and that violates ethical rules."

"I couldn't help it. I do beg your forgiveness. I'll take responsibility for my actions," Maha uttered the words quietly.

"I forgive you this time. When I was younger, I had difficulty resisting young attractive female patients ..., " he coughed and then continued. "There are indications that we are talking about a patient with a severe personality disorder. I have been following this case for a long period. Is there anything in the history of his illness that you haven't told us?" Dr. Benjamin said to Maha with a tighter voice, "I need to know. It is in the best interest of all of us."

Maha blushed and said shyly, "At the last session, he was completely possessed by the image of *superman*. He fell into some kind of trance. I am guessing by the way he was talking, his gestures and the unusual glow in his eyes, that there was his other Self present. He seemed to be real for a moment. I thought it was all in my mind until he started talking about the Judgement Day and the Jerusalem prophet who was about to arrive. He was very convincing."

"Yes, convincing," Dr. Benjamin took a long breath and continued, "Maha, you knew that he had pathological personality traits and that his pretty face could anytime turn into a demonic face. Next time be careful. Go home. I'll call you a taxi."

"Love was stronger," Maha said and went towards the door.

Dr. Benjamin asked Abdul to walk Maha to the taxi. We were alone. I said, "By the way, if they were lovers, why did he attack her?"

"He was to be healed. However, Shamil couldn't accept the illness and confront the unreal image."

"I have to say that I almost suspected Abdul when he showed up at the door like a lightning bolt out of a blue sky."

"I wasn't sure about him, either."

"Don't you think we should let our superiors know about the attack on Maha?"

"There is no need. No one is here."

"Are you sure? Could Shamil get into the hospital?"

"The guard would stop him. Hadassah is one of the highest-security hospitals. He only wanted to take revenge on Maha for exposing him. Let's go home. I'll take you."

THE SUICIDE OF THE GYPSY WOMAN

The rain that had started a few days ago and threatened to sweep us away with the blustery showers, began to slow, and the citizens returned to the streets of the deserted city. By the end of the week the skies had cleared. Everyone was discussing where to get away and spend a restful weekend.

The case of Shamil was almost forgotten when something else happened, creating an epilogue to the story about the Jerusalem prophet. It was about the end of the workday when I got a call from the Head of the Psychiatric Department asking me to keep the Gypsy woman in our department during the weekend because their staff wasn't on duty. This was an unprecedented problem that even Dr. Benjamin couldn't solve. As our department was under the Psychiatric Department and it was too late to ask the hospital manager to intervene, we couldn't agree on who would be on duty. So on Friday afternoon, the first sunny day after the storm, the eccentric Gypsy woman was put under our care. She was diagnosed with insanity as the result of providence. As I spent my days off with Ibrahim, the responsibility fell on me.

I cooly received the news about the Gypsy woman coming, and knowing that such cases are usually predictable, I quietly continued working. We put the Gypsy woman in a separate room and gave her a Bible that she asked to read to our astonishment. We gave her the old Dr. Benjamin's Bible that he kept together with the Talmud and the Koran in his desk drawer.

I was about to complete my review of the medical records, but before I could finish, I heard loud cries coming from the Gypsy woman's room. I ran towards the room. The Gypsy woman[71] was standing with her arms apart crying out like a prophet, "But when you see the ABOMINATION OF DESOLATION standing where it should not be…"[72] I entered the room. She stopped briefly and looked straight at me with her piercing eyes, pointing her finger at my face, "His destiny is in your hands."

---

[71] There is a small number of Gypsies called Domari Gypsies in Jerusalem. In Israel they mostly speak Arabic, some of them Hebrew and a few of them English. The older generation speaks a dialect of Domari. The majority of them proclaim themselves Muslims, and a few of them Christians.

[72] https://biblehub.com/context/mark/13.htm.

I managed to calm her down. I sat her down on the bed and handed the Bible to her. She probably remained in that position until the guard came to stay with her for the night. When I woke up in the morning, I heard him yelling, "Doctor, hurry up!"

When I entered the room, I saw the Gypsy woman hanging from the ceiling lamp with a bed sheet around her neck. The guard took her down and laid her on the bed. I came closer to the head of the bed. There was a page torn from the Bible that ended with the words of the Gospel of Mark, "And then if anyone says to you, 'Behold, here is the Christ'; or, 'Behold, He is there'; do not believe him; for false Christs and false prophets will arise, and will show signs and wonders, in order to lead astray, if possible, the elect. "[73]

I closed the Bible and tried for a pulse on the Gypsy woman's neck to see if she was dead. The Gypsy woman was still warm. I ran my hands down her chest touching the pendant on her necklace. It resembled an amulet of an unusual triangular-pyramidal shape. It was like a sorcerer's ball of light in the form of a star. I was attracted to its exquisite glow. Hearing the steps and the guard's voice coming down the hall, I didn't have time to look at the amulet closely enough. I quickly

[73] https://biblehub.com/context/mark/13.htm. Ibid.

grabbed it and put it in the inner pocket of my purse. I called the ambulance and headed towards my room.

ON THE EVE OF THE HAJJ[74] HOLIDAY

The rest of the month passed uneventfully. My daily life was slowly returning to normal and David returned as well. He seemed somehow different, silent and pensive, indicating that he wanted to be left alone as he worked for the highest good. I tried not to ask him too much, until one day on the way to work, I saw on the front page of the newspaper some disturbing news. It concerned the long term secret plan of the Radical Jewish Movement to build a Jewish temple on the site of the Mosque of Omar. The plan was to be announced soon and implemented if the Israeli government approved it during its last session of the year.

Arriving at work, I ran in to see David. I entered his office breathless, waving the newspaper, "David, have you read? You wouldn't believe... "

David interrupted me and responded calmly, "I know, Antonija. It's not as easy as it may seem."

"What are you saying?"

"Building the temple would mean the destruction of the existing temple, the Mosque of Omar, and perhaps, the nearby Al-Aqsa Mosque[75] as well, which could lead to Muslim retaliation. The conflict has deep historical roots. I don't have time to explain."

"I know, I read."

"Antonija, may we meet after lunch at our place next to the Chagall windows?"

"Sure."

Waiting for David, I was thinking about historical stories about Israel that I liked to read while gazing at the Chagall windows. It was obvious that he was impressed by Biblical motifs. I was standing under the tall stained glass window with the red background and the images of the crown on the top and the lion at the bottom. The symbolism was very indicative. It alluded to the anointed king, the Messiah, who would come from the tribe of Judah as it was heralded in Jacob's Testament in Genesis[76]. I was thinking about

---

[75] Al-Aqsa Mosque is located in the Old City of Jerusalem. It dates back to 709 A.D. It was built on top of the Temple Mount or Al-Aqsa compound that remains a constant point of dispute in the Palestinian-Israeli conflict.

[76] "Judah, your brothers shall praise you; your hand shall be on

the symbolism of the image when David approached me. I was listening to him in disbelief when he uttered this, "Antonija, I couldn't talk about it there. It's not just about building the new temple, but the new king who could sit in the temple of God. Though he wouldn't come from God, he would proclaim himself to be God and would have Divine attributes."

It went through my mind that it would not be Jesus, this long-awaited Messiah heralded by the Old Testament texts.

"The Antichrist?" I exclaimed.

"Antonija, it's better not to pronounce his name. He would be preceded by many prophets. They would speak in His name, perform miracles and mislead the ignorant."

"Oh my God! When do you expect him?"

"I am not sure. I think it might happen after the plan is approved by the Israeli government. The problem is that its last session is on the day of the Hajj, the major Muslim religious holiday that falls during the Christmas and New Year holidays. It's dangerous if

---

the neck of your enemies; your father's sons shall bow down to you. Judah is a lion's whelp; from the prey, my son, you have gone up. He couches, he lies down as a lion, and as a lion, who dares rouse him up? The scepter shall not depart from Judah, nor the ruler's staff from between his feet, until Shiloh comes, and to him shall be the obedience of the peoples." https://biblehub.com/context/genesis/49-8.htm.

the government adopts the decision at that moment, as it may lead to a Muslim rebellion not only in Israel but across the globe. There is not much time left, only two weeks."

I let my mind wander recalling grandmother Lucija. I revived my Liburnian spirit and instinctively felt powerful. I felt the voice in my heart. I heard my grandmother's words about the heroic deed I was chosen to perform by Divine Providence. I should go forward in her image with trust and help her in the battle to save people's souls on Earth.

CLOSE ENCOUNTER

The long-awaited day, the Hajj Holiday, drew near. It was one of the most important days for Muslims all over the world. They would give anything to fulfill their wish to see Mecca on that day. Those who stayed in Jerusalem celebrated by going on a pilgrimage to the Mosque of Omar. They paid homage to the Holy City, a sacred site in Islamic tradition.

I was listening to the last news from the session of the Israeli government. The government, to my great surprise, adopted the plan to build a Jewish temple on the site of the Mosque of Omar.

I was sitting like a stone following the latest news when I suddenly saw on the screen the image of the imposing Mosque of Omar rising above the walls of the Old City. Its golden dome was shining in a display of color that looked like fireflies amplified by glaring fireworks. Then there appeared the image of the nearby square with the words of a reporter informing the citizens of Jerusalem, "Today, when the eyes of the world are on Mecca, thousands of worshippers are pouring towards the Mosque of Omar. It is said that the prophet appeared in front of it out of nowhere. There are Muslims, Christians and Jews among the worshippers. Citizens are asked to stay home. The Armed guards are located at the main entrance of the mosque to prevent anyone from entering."

The image disappeared, and then the phone rang. It was David. He said he was waiting for me at the door downstairs. I grabbed my coat and purse and went towards the exit. I gave a nod to the guard. He pointed to the black Mercedes from where David was waving.

"A luxury car," I said surprised.

"It's a government vehicle for emergencies. We shall take a pass and hope that we can slip through to the first rows."

"David, were you aware of the prophet?"

"I'll be honest with you, I was surprised. I felt disbelief when I heard what my colleague said. It was about two hours ago."

"Why didn't you tell me?"

"I was waiting for the official announcement. I didn't want to tell you without reason."

"Where do we go?"

"Towards the first rows where Ibrahim is waiting for us."

We arrived at the entrance to the Old City in a few minutes. They let our Mercedes through immediately. The guard even took charge of us and moved us forward.

We went towards the first rows where Ibrahim greeted me with a warm handshake. He quickly told me that the crowd had been gathering for about an hour, waiting for the proclamation of the prophet.

A medley of voices, some poor unfortunate souls crying and the wailing of repenters, filled the air. I held Ibrahim's hand. David stood behind me. I was fully protected. I felt restless, looking for the face of the prophet. When he turned towards the gathering, I was startled to discover that it was Ishmael, the young man from the photo in the school newspaper of the school run by the United Nations at the Shatila Palestinian refugee camp.

"Brothers and sisters, I came to share the great news about Jerusalem descending from Heaven."

"To the Glory of it, to the Glory of it!" the crowd was yelling.

The prophet then turned towards the mosque cheering in His name. The crowd was nudging each other to see who the prophet was addressing.

"For behold, he will create new heavens and a new

earth; and the former things will not be remembered or come to mind."[77]

The cries were heard. The crowd started raising images. I stood on my tiptoe to see the image that the man in the row in front of me was waving. I looked closer and I recognized Abdulah, the Jordanian physician with whom I traveled by plane to Jerusalem. It crossed my mind that maybe he was the informer we were looking for. I was even more shocked when I saw a figure on the image that resembled the apparition that appeared to me in the Beirut hills. It was that same figure with deep-set, translucent, black, hypnotic eyes and skin coated in gold.

The crowd was yelling, "Jesus! Jesus! Mahdi! Mahdi![78] Messiah! Messiah![79] "

"I couldn't believe my eyes," I asked David, "who do you see?"

"The Messiah."

---

[77] The exact quote from the Bible, "For behold, I create new heavens and a new earth; and the former things will not be remembered or come to mind." https://biblehub.com/context/isaiah/65-17.htm.

[78] In Islamic eschatology – the Savior who will appear before the end of the world and restore justice and equity on Earth.

[79] In early Jewish apocalypses – the Savior and redeemer who will establish the Kingdom of peace and justice at the end of the world.

"And you, Ibrahim?"

"Mahdi."

"Oh my God, am I the only one who sees Him?"

The images that were waving like flags in the wind depicted a faceless figure with a cold expression, surrounded by the same glittering light that covered me in the hut in the Beirut hills. Then I heard a voice from the distance, "You see the face of God. He who has seen me has seen the Father."[80]

Then a dead silence fell. My restless thoughts were interrupted by inaudible heartbeats. I came to my senses recognizing the voice from within. It was the silent voice of Self.

"The Devil wants to delude you. No man has seen the face of God."

I turned to David and whispered, "Do I see the Antichrist?"

David said in confirmation, "Unbelievable! Only you can see Him in the proper light."

The prophet continued talking to a crowd, "And the former things will not be remembered and the temple will be destroyed!"

I was listening carefully to the prophet's words. I was confused. It was not only that I couldn't find the link between Mihovil and Ishmael, Abraham's

---

[80] Cf. John 1:1,14; 14,9.

unpromised son from whom the Arab nations descended. But also I couldn't find the link between the prophet and the one whom the prophet was addressing, who was the one who announced the building of a new temple[81] on the same site where it was before the Romans destroyed it in 70 A.D. He was supposed to rebuild the holy site for the Jews. Something was wrong here. It crossed my mind that he may be of some other ancestry, but I wasn't sure.

A powerful surge of energy overtook my body. It was rising from my feet to the top of my head. I was suddenly off balance, pulled by the deadly energy field. The prophet stared into my eyes while focusing all his power on me. His diabolic eyes appeared to grow darker as he focused menacingly on me. As I was drawn into his eyes, I suddenly saw Mihovil's figure smiling at me. I swayed slightly as I was lifted up from the ground. I wanted to run towards the prophet, but Ibrahim pulled me back. He stood in front of me protecting me with his body. I uttered a scream of fear trying to hold Ibrahim back, but it was too late. He was pulled by the prophet's energy and sucked into a

---

[81] According to the Biblical records, it is believed that Solomon's Temple was the First Temple in Jerusalem. The expulsion of the Jewish people is traditionally dated from the destruction of the Temple. The building of the Temple began about 968 B.C. It is mentioned in the Old Testament: I Kings 5:15-5:32.

violent whirlpool. It lasted only a few seconds. I was highly distraught. I left my dear friend without even looking at him. He passed away giving his life for me, as he prophesied.

A hush fell over the atmosphere. I suddenly started rising up from the ground. I was lifted by the rhythm of the song that I heard reverberating in my right ear. I thought it might be a song coming by waves of light from the depths of the Universe. Strangely, it was my favorite song, sung by Pandit Sati. Then a vision appeared to everyone there which made their faces beam with joy. In the same place where the prophet stood, a shadow now appeared which became an elongated female figure followed by the figures of my Liburnian Goddesses.

"Antonija, don't believe him! Don't believe him, Jerusalem!" the voices of the Goddesses filled the air hovering over the city walls.

Then a menacing shout was heard, "The former things will not be remembered and the temple and the city will be destroyed!"

When I heard the prophet's words, I realized that he would mentally capture the crowd.

I came down to the ground and stood in front of the prophet looking into his eyes. The figures of the Goddesses were floating over me while I was re-energizing. I lifted my arm, pointing my finger at the prophet's eyes. A warmth overwhelmed me like a tidal wave of bliss. The rush of energy started spreading stronger and stronger through my arm and seemed to burst through my tingling fingers. The prophet pulled back. He was becoming smaller and smaller until he completely vanished. Before that, he managed to say, "I'll see you again!"

DAVID CONTINUED WITH BRISK steps towards the Golden Gate[82]. While he was walking through the gate, it felt like time sped up. A part of me split and flew over the City Walls towards the Mount of Olives. I turned around to the sunny pine grove leaving David behind me. I could see him for some time carrying my body in his arms.

When he disappeared from my sight, I felt like I was lifted up on angel's wings. Then I vanished into the vastness of spacetime. It was a unique continuum consisting of a myriad of parallel worlds. I was observing them like an Oversoul that was carrying the imprints of our all-encompassing being at all levels of existence. Being aware of myself as one part of it,

---

[82] The Golden Gate on the east walls of the Old City dates back to 1541 A.D.

I could have chosen when to experience a particular part of myself. As soon as I felt that way, I entered a powerful energy vortex. I was swept away by a large light wave and thrown into interspace.

I floated through it like a spot in the vast ocean of nothingness until the Earth appeared in outline. I observed the Earth with spiritual eyes, catching the flickering rays of a gentle illuminating light. It looked like a morning drop of dew in which the entirety of the Universe was reflected. Within the reach of its aura, I felt I was listening to the heartbeat of the Soul of the Universe and experiencing the joy of the magical moment of Oneness.

The experience lasted for a few seconds. The feeling of bliss soon gave way to restlessness. In a twinkling, I was carried on invisible wings beyond eyesight of the Earth. The light was fading in the distance as the darkness took over, brought by a deadly wave from the opposite direction. With it a translucent, black, hypnotic eye came out of the abyss.

A shudder passed through me at the sight of the apparition. Riding on the Earth's coat-tails, I was looking at it, trying to slip away from its eye while being slowly engulfed by it. The more I watched it, the more it accelerated. The eye suddenly started spinning so fast that I felt giddy. It seemed to me to be the wheel of karma spinning. When it stopped, I saw a faceless, man-like being approaching, emerging from the all-pervasive blackness. His appearance filled me with disgust. I suddenly had an image that in one of the infinite dimensions of time he would be crowned. Although I couldn't determine exactly where I was, in some incomprehensible way, I felt bound to him by fate.

I was almost completely sucked into the abyss, when I heard a voice which seemed to come from a barely visible light, "Let go of fear. He cannot harm you." I finally realized that by swallowing me, the frightening being swallowed the entire Earth. The wings that had been carrying me dropped away and the Earth came back into my vision. It was as though I was a silent observer, not the cause of the event, but the one who altered the flow of time. Time was going on right now – as an eternal NOW, where future and past meet – at a historical moment that I was witnessing. Before I would go back to time, I heard for the last time a voice whispering in the rhythm of the melancholy music of the Universe, "Go back to the Source. It will provide you with inexhaustible strength. Stop the Devil before he seals the Earthmen's fate."

I REGAINED CONSCIOUSNESS AT the hotel room in Jerusalem. David was sitting next to me. I had the shivers, and I felt light-headed. David said that I was not safe at the hotel. I managed to pull myself together and I looked for Khalil's Rabbi's number.

"Here is the number," I gave it to David and then collapsed.

I woke up the next day at the Rabbi's apartment. I was surrounded by unknown objects. Everything indicated that it was the Rabbi's apartment. I could see it for myself when a real Rabbi appeared in front of me. I thought I had seen him before. I recognized him when David joined us. It was the Rabbi with notably wilted cheeks, whose image I saw reflected in the small shop's mirror in the vicinity of the restaurant on Cardo Street where I had dinner with David.

David turned to me and said, "Antonija, Rabbi Yitzhak is our friend. He is going to help us through his friends so that you can leave Jerusalem as soon as possible. You are not safe here anymore."

"Are you sending me far away again?"

"Khalil notified us that we could expect to see the prophet in New York. We don't know what he is planning."

"I don't understand. Why do you think that? What do you expect from me?"

"Antonija," David said, after a short break, "we all witnessed how in a spectacular way you overpowered the prophet. We fear his revenge."

He cannot harm me, I thought while activating the primordial beauty and power of the Liburnian Goddess within myself.

"We need your help to track down this self-proclaimed prophet," David continued. "You will join our ranks."

"The Secret Service ranks?" I looked at him with wide open eyes.

"You are already connected with us."

Khalil and his peers... What else could I have expected? How else could all these trips and study courses be accounted for? It's better to accept it, I said to myself.

"We prepared your papers and arranged a continuation of your sabbatical year at New York University Medical Center[83]. Here is the number of your supervisor. Her name is Elza. She is a psychotherapist. You can rely on her."

"When do I leave?"

"In two hours."

I silently nodded to David in assent. I felt sorry to

---

[83] New York Langone Medical Center is located in the heart of Manhattan and includes the New York School of Medicine, founded in 1841 and several hospitals.

leave this warm and simple man. First and foremost, I felt sorry not to have time to say good-bye to my dear co-workers. I hoped they would understand the circumstances and wouldn't take offense at my leaving so abruptly.

I quickly changed clothes and packed my belongings. Then I went to say good-bye to the Rabbi. I bowed to him and expressed my gratitude for his kindness. He walked me to the door and said a loving "Shalom".

David went with me to the taxi stand and we said our good-byes.

"It will be our victory!"

David hugged me. He took his skullcap off and put it on my head. He kissed my hand and said in a friendly tone, "You only need a skullcap to be a real Rabbi. "Shalom," Antonija!"

AT TWO O'CLOCK IN the afternoon, I left Jerusalem. I set out for New York, a world political center, to thwart the next step of the prophet.

LIGHTS

OF

NEW

YORK

———

IV

RECEPTION IN
NEW YORK

The lights of New York appeared on the horizon, glittering on the tall skyscrapers like the beacons for the airplanes that were constantly flying over them. The pilot announced our landing in New York John F. Kennedy Airport. As soon as I set foot on American soil I felt relieved. I was hoping that I would discard the old me and put on a new face the moment I landed.

As I got off the airplane, a young, nice-looking woman met me. I knew it was Elza. She approached with her hand outstretched and gave me a warm American hug. We went downtown in an oversized, silver, metallic Ford. We stopped in front of a luxury hotel, The Envoy Club. It occupied the first seven floors of the twenty-two-story, residential building near the historic Murray Hill[84] in Manhattan. It was an

---

[84] Murray Hill is a Manhattan neighborhood on the East side of Manhattan. Its first family, Mary and Robert Murray, built their house on a hill in the 18th century. It became popularly known as Murray Hill.

Apartment Hotel that normally hosted high-ranking business guests. Their regular customers also were visitors to New York University Medical Center who liked to stay there because of the proximity to the center.

Elza accompanied me to my room. It was a neat room with warm colors. A comfortable red plush armchair was placed prominently in the room next to the tall wide glass windows with a view of the road. On the little table next to the armchair were a lit lamp and a glass, obviously left for a weary traveler.

The morning was approaching. Elza left me to unpack and sleep for a few hours to be ready for tomorrow to meet some of her co-workers. The knocking on the door woke me up around ten o'clock. It was the most beautiful, welcome breakfast I could wish for. I truly enjoyed the fragrant pastry. The macaroon cookies, filled with fresh raspberries, rose cream, fresh Asian cherry fruit and decorated with bright red rose petals, impressed me most of all. Biting into the cookie was like tasting love. The aromatic rose petal with a delicate scent brought back memories of the Liburnian Goddess Anzotika. It crossed my mind that maybe through this secret signal someone was sending me love.

The telephone interrupted my reverie. Elza wished me a good morning and said that her co-worker Arnold was waiting for me downstairs. I didn't expect a call so early. I thought she would let me rest a little longer, but I realized that my first day of work would be busy. I would have to adjust to the environment of hard working Americans and learn how to reconcile work with pleasure.

I cleared the table and put the leftovers on the plate. I put on a short coat and sports pants and went downstairs where an attractive man with hair pulled up high over his head and slicked down with brilliantine was waiting. He smiled, showing a nice row of white teeth. He sounded like a girl when he spoke.

Arnold was a little bit taller than I. He was much younger. He was around twenty. In his youthful appearance, he reminded me of Mihovil. I stared at him. He had the same look in his eyes as Mihovil had when I first saw him: I could feel his black eyes, darker than the darkness of the Universe penetrating deeply into my soul. Our eyes met briefly: I felt an irresistible attraction remembering how I could lose myself in the love of Mihovil's eyes. I noticed a slight discomfort in Arnold's attitude as he looked down.

On the way to the hospital Arnold was explaining non-standard treatment therapies, the most effective for non-psychotic mental disorders like stress and anxiety. He invited me to join him tomorrow at an art therapy session at the Psychiatric Department where he was doing his medical residency while studying simultaneously at the New York Academy of Art[85]. He talked about his colleagues in the department who were writing a lot of research papers to maintain academic standing at the department while doing clinical training. Listening to chatty Arnold, I arrived sooner than I expected at the hospital complex right on the coast of the East River. Thanks to him I overcame the first feeling of crisis that usually overtook me when coming to a new environment. Maybe the cheerfulness of the rest of the three colleagues was the reason I was able to accept it so easily. They welcomed me with applause and a sweet, fruit cocktail.

Elza, Ellen and Michael were different at first sight from the Israeli "police" doctors. There was a relaxed atmosphere without any secrecy in the department. The hospital staff seemed to be young with a perspective fully devoted to scientific research and patient care. The high level of their achievements indicated that this was a very modern, sophisticated research center. Moreover, what made it important was the location of the department, on the East River next to prominent buildings like the United Nations. By coincidence

---

[85] The New York Academy of Art is a private graduate school established in 1982.

or not, my office had a view of these buildings. My eyes took in the beautiful scenery of the bridge in the distance connecting Queens and Manhattan with the bright blue sky stretching out before it.

THE ART THERAPY

G aining insight into the psyche had always been
a challenge to me. When I started working at
the Psychiatric Department, I wanted to get to know
the world of mentally disturbed people. It was most
visible in the clear expression of their paintings that
reflected universal love rising out of the depths of
the human being and permeated with the primordial
substance of the Universe.

Arnold drew my attention to the painting of a
patient with borderline personality disorder which
exhibited a strong feeling of loneliness. To solve
loneliness, these patients often indulge in fantasy. I
approached the young man with a gloomy expression
on his face. He had melancholy green eyes and brown
hair flecked with gray. John was leaning towards the
painting stroking the canvas with a paint brush. He
didn't look back when I put my hand on his shoulder.
He was engrossed in his world, immersed in the beauty
of color. In the painting that I was looking at out of the

corner of my eye, he seemed to be thematizing himself by creating the space for fantasy and symbolic content, bringing us into the world of the subconscious.

Love was significantly expressed in the painting. There was a heart in the middle with the roots below and a wide crown of the tree above. Its symbolism reflected the "tree of life" that in many beliefs and myths connected the Kingdom of Earth and the Kingdom of Heaven. It was the symbol of a life force, a psychic energy necessary for healing – the energy of the heart, whose flame could be enkindled only by love.

I approached John asking what he wanted to convey with the painting. He said he wanted to express feelings of sublime beauty. It was obvious to me that he had painted with the flame of the heart in mind that was taking strength from eternity, revealing the concept of love.

Through art therapy, John had managed to balance his psychic energy which now allowed him to be healed. His renewed life force offered him the opportunity to feel love. John became aware of himself as an artist, and like the mythological bird the Phoenix, he arose from the ashes to continue living and creating.

THE PLAY OF LIGHT
AND SHADOW

In the silence of the early evening, my room was dimly lit with light reaching into all corners of the room. An amazing play of light and shadow created a special emotional atmosphere which added a mystical dimension.

Having in mind John's painting from the art shop, I strode into the world of imagination. The painting aroused in me a primeval longing that emerged from my need to reach spiritual heights. It was an erotic longing for a reunion with love – the Platonic eternal longing for Beauty. The Liburnian Goddess Anzotika was an embodiment of power to me that would help me climb to these heights and return to my primordial nature.

I listened for a moment to the silence of a timeless beauty. I could see a figure embraced by light and shadow hovering in front of me. It was reflected in the window bathed in the reddish light of the sunset. The scent of Mihovil's breath filled the room. I recalled my old dreams in order to allow the longing I had for him to arise. I still longed for the gleam in his eyes and could feel my fingers tracing a gentle shadow on his lips. I ran towards him to feel the moment of eternal unity. As though my soul caressed my own shadow, I experienced the ecstasy of unity, recognizing him in myself and myself in him. With a sigh of our shadows, our souls were rising like a sublime light into the vastness of the Universe, two unified mind-body souls of the Universe.

I was overpowered by sleep. The figure hidden behind the window wings was fading away. His shadow was dragging behind him until it wandered somewhere far away.

AN UNEXPECTED ENCOUNTER

During the mid-morning therapies at the Psychiatric Department, Elza and I went to lunch at the exclusive Sheraton Russel Hotel on Park Avenue. Elza wanted to show me a New Yorker's New York, as they referred to the neighborhood next to 34th Street with a lot of shops and restaurants. For that very reason she chose a luxury hotel for lunch among the many other restaurants in the neighborhood. I soon realized that wasn't the only reason for her choice when I saw Khalil in a hotel lobby. He was elegant as usual, his suit blending perfectly with the stylish mahogany English furniture, sitting in an armchair carved into the shape of a swan.

"Look, look who is here," Khalil ran into my embrace.

"Welcome, my dear friend!" I took his hands nodding to Elza. Elza looked back at me signaling with her eyes that I was free. I was delighted. I couldn't wait to finish lunch so I could devote myself to my faithful friend and spend at least an afternoon with him, or for as long as he would be in New York.

At lunch we talked while sampling exquisite English dishes, perfectly in style with the traditional English atmosphere. Elza left us soon after she had a coffee and only Khalil remained to further our conversation. I gave him a suspicious look. I couldn't believe my eyes. He had suddenly appeared like a ghost from a bottle. Silence loomed between us as in the moments when you meet an old friend and want to tell him a lot, but don't know where to start. Khalil broke the uneasy silence with a cheerful smile on his face.

"Antonija, I am staying only a short while in New York. I have something urgent to do and I also wanted to see you."

"I am glad," I said after a short pause, "my best friend a spy? Why didn't you tell me?"

"Antonija, my role is beyond my personal interest. You will understand one day. You have to trust me," Khalil turned to me.

"I trust you, though I don't know why, as I have already told you," I said in a calmer tone.

Khalil looked at me with raised eyebrows as though he wanted to let me know there was something important to tell me. I was wondering if I wanted to know it. I had been very pleased by his attention ever since the first day. Nevertheless, I was upset by the feeling that arose with Khalil's sudden visit, a weird feeling of anxiety that filled the air. The unsolved case of Mihovil's disappearance was floating between us, and I was waiting with bated breath to hear some news about my love. Mihovil's image danced before my eyes when I heard Khalil's words, "We can expect our Jerusalem prophet Ishmael to appear at the United Nations."

I wanted to hear anything but that. No word about Mihovil. Only a few prosaic words about his double, announcing a dramatic outcome in New York. I made a face just thinking of Ishmael.

"How do you know?" I asked Khalil, frowning.

"During the intelligence gathering process we scanned the voice of an employee at the Diplomatic Mission of Israel on the East River."

"You mean to say by spying?" I interrupted Khalil.

"Collecting information about the employees at the Diplomatic Missions in a host country is a standard diplomatic procedure. An employee of the Diplomatic Mission of Israel mentioned Ishmael during a conversation."

"It could be anyone by this name. Where do you see a link to the Jerusalem prophet?" I asked Khalil.

"His name was mentioned in the context of the

shadow government, a unique World Government whose establishment should be supervised by the United Nations."

"Ishmael appeared last time in the front of the Mosque of Omar heralding the coming of a new king who would sit in the rebuilt Temple of Solomon in Jerusalem. Had it happened, what implications could it have on world events?"

"The point is that Israel's rebuilt temple was supposed to become the center of the world, the center of the World Government."

"Could you explain this?"

"The Jews were chosen by God to prepare the world for the coming of the Messiah. By his coronation in a new temple on the site of today's Mosque of Omar, the Jews would be granted an earthly kingdom and would take over the world."

"Should the one who sits in the temple be of Jewish blood?"

"I am not sure. Ishmael heralded the coming of a new king who would sit in the Temple of Jerusalem. According to the Old Testament stories, Ishmael was Abraham's first son, but not the promised Son of God. Ishmael was the father of the Arab nation. The promised Son of God was Isaac, Ishmael's half-brother. The Jews descended from Isaac. The Jews believe that

the Messiah would be a Jew, and Muslims believe that
Mahdi would be an Arab. The new ruler of the World
Government should be recognized by most Jews and
Arabs as their Messiah. But both nations are on the
wrong track."

"Of what blood would a new king be?"

"It is not known to me. The new king should bring
a reconciliation between the Jews and the Arabs
and take over the world by establishing the World
Government."

*The apparition from the Beirut hills? A deep-set,
translucent, black, hypnotic eye? I can't believe it*, I said
to myself.

"Antonija, I came to warn you. Whoever contacts
you with any news about Ishmael, call me immediately.
I'll need your help. We can stop him together."

I understand, I murmured to myself.

After we left the restaurant, we walked slowly
towards Fifth Avenue and the Empire State Building[86].
We didn't go further because it was almost the time
of departure of Khalil's airplane.

I calmed down after the first few steps walking in
the shadow of the trees. When we came to the famous

---

[86] The Empire State Building is a 102-story skyscraper in
Midtown Manhattan with an unobstructed panoramic view
of New York City and beyond.

Empire State Building with its tower that seemed to be swinging under the clouds, Khalil suddenly stopped. I heard a short ringtone from the pocket of his trousers. I knew it meant he was leaving. He kissed me strongly on my forehead and hugged me tightly. He went away into the unknown, leaving me at the mercy of the city that would welcome a woman newcomer who would boldly knock on its door, ready to tackle the greatest challenges and temptations of her life.

THE VISITORS
IN THE OFFICE

For the rest of the week there was a lively discussion at the Psychiatric Department of the New York University Medical Center about the results of the recent Conference of the World Federation of Mental Health. The most lively participants were Ellen and Michael. They competed with each other as to who would be the most convincing in the clinical descriptions of a middle-aged woman, the new patient in the department whose treatment had not been decided.

Bertha was a Professor of Russian Literature at New York University. She had a sharp, almost a genius mind. She was a hope of her generation. She had fallen into severe depression and painted herself into a corner. Elza presumed that Bertha's last act of throwing her clothes on the streets of New York was her final step before suicide. It was important to Elza to hear my opinion about the case. She gave me comprehensive documentation of the history of the disease.

I wanted to spend time reviewing the case on Friday after work. I entered the office when the phone rang. The doorman told me that two visitors were on their way to my office. I straightened my hair and put on lipstick. I was looking at the door, but the door handle wasn't moving. I stood quietly listening attentively to the steps that were coming from the nearby fire escape. The steps were getting louder. I opened the door to see who was approaching on the stairs when a hand interrupted my reaching for the door handle. A black glove was on the left hand of the attacker. He grabbed my wrists behind my back holding them tightly while putting his right hand over my mouth. He pushed me into the office. I was gasping for breath trying to resist, when unbearable pain overwhelmed me spreading throughout the body. I was left speechless by fear. Waiting for the next move of the attacker, my whole life unwound before my eyes like a movie. I thought he would kill me.

Then I saw another attacker. He was short and unimpressive. He had a cocked hat. He looked sophisticated in an elegant suit. He gave me a despised expression, his deep, cold blue eyes glaring. I was scared he would hit me. But when he approached me, his eyes seemed to waver. My sixth sense told me the attackers wanted information from me. No sooner had this thought crossed my mind when another attacker took a photo out of his suit and started waving it. He brought it closer to my face, and I was perturbed to recognize the face of Ishmael. Then the attacker started talking in my ear. He demanded to know about Mihovil's whereabouts or else I would be hurt. Then steps were heard coming from the operating room on the second floor. By the sound of the high heels I knew they were from a woman. They were approaching the room. In the meantime, the first attacker released my arms. Before he escaped, he threatened to kill me if I told anyone about our encounter.

The door closed and I ran towards the wash-bowl. I quickly removed the suspicious traces of the attackers. I adjusted my scrub and sat at the table. I gathered my last thread of strength to stay focused on the documentation of the history of Bertha's disease. I had a feeling that Elza was coming. When she entered the office, she looked at me in astonishment asking if everything was all right. I said I had a headache and would get back to work as soon as it passed.

AN INVITATION
TO THE OPERA

The breakfast, delivered early in the morning on the first day of the spring to the door of my hotel room, made my day feel just as it had when I first arrived in New York. With the breakfast came an invitation to the Metropolitan Opera[87], the renowned Franco Zeffirelli's production of *La Traviata*[88].

I wasn't very happy with the selection, however, I couldn't miss a rare opportunity to visit one of the world's most famous opera houses. Elza had persuaded me to visit the opera. She said that it was an amazingly beautiful production.

The day of the opera house approached. I picked a reddish dress with a golden waist belt on Elza's

[87] The Metropoltan Opera is a leading U.S. opera company founded in 1880.

[88] Franco Zeffirelli's production of the famous Giuseppe Verdi's opera. Franco Zeffirelli (1923-2019) was an Italian director and producer of operas, films and television. *La Traviata* by Giuseppe Verdi was premiered in Venice at La Fenice Opera House on March 6, 1853.

advice. Elza was a true lady and she wanted me to be elegant too.

I spent the afternoon getting ready. I was almost late. I came to the opera when the bell rang for the third time announcing the start of the play.

I sat breathless in the loge seat and looked around. I noticed the vacant seat next to me. There was a bright blue rose with gentle buds on it. It was an unexpected gift. It crossed my mind, *Wasn't Mihovil the only one who knew that I liked blue roses?* I wished the rose was from him. Then the doorman approached and said carefully, "The gentleman who left the rose wishes you a good evening."

I couldn't contain my disappointment. I beckoned to the doorman to move away. I tried to enjoy the play with the famous Greek-German soprano and a handsome Italian tenor. Neither the choral accompaniment, nor the glamorous stage that seemed to faithfully conjure up the image of the Paris Salon with the rich costumes and colorful balloons, nor the magnificent lights invigorating the atmosphere with glitter and glory, could dispel my wandering thoughts.

Indeed, I didn't wait for the end of the play. I went back to my hotel room. I turned the light on and threw off my camel-hair coat. I clumsily gripped my purse. It fell on the floor. My makeup fell on the floor. The little mirror was the last item that fell out together with the pendant of an unusual shape. I took it in my hand. I opened my hand, looking into the glassy point of the triangle pyramid structure. A gentle light started emanating from its center. I couldn't take my eyes off it. The light grew stronger. The intoxicating scent of lilies filled my nostrils. I was delightfully dazed. Once again I was gazing in disbelief into the translucent black eye. Its appearance vaguely recalled to me the unearthly object that I found in Jerusalem on the neck of the eccentric Gypsy woman. I wanted to merge with its increasing radiance.

Turning around, I was looking for the presence of my love, for the beam of love that would alleviate the feeling of inner unrest and concealed fear that was following me since the day of his disappearance. I was calling for Mihovil's image. I was no longer sure whether it was real or an illusion. I remembered how my soul trembled in his presence. I didn't want anything but the day to come as soon as possible when our spell of love would come to life again.

SIGNS OF MELANCHOLIA

The days were passing in their usual monotonous way. Waiting for Mihovil, I became repeatedly overwhelmed with sorrow. The first signs of melancholia emerged with the first rains of spring. It usually happened quietly and unannounced, lurking and waiting for the next innocent victim.

Elza decided to take matters into her own hands. She offered me a more widespread color therapy program instead of drug therapy. One day she invited me to her room.

"Antonija, we therapists sometimes need therapy as well. There is nothing unusual in this. However, your case is more mysterious in the way that it is related to the inexplicable events."

"So you know."

"I made inquiries. Antonija, were you waiting for your Mihovil at the theater?" Elza asked me.

"I have directed all my efforts towards finding him,

from my hometown of Preko in Croatia via Lebanon, to Israel, and all the way to New York. I was hoping we would meet again. But I am not sure anymore whether the invitation to the opera was from him or his double."

"His double? Could you please clarify, Antonija?"

"Since my recent stay in Beirut, I have been seeing a young man whose appearance is related to so many mysterious events. He is following me like some uninvited apparition. The anxiety that I feel may be a result of pent-up guilt over the loss of my loved one. The young man, though he resembles Mihovil in appearance, doesn't resemble him in his soul."

"How do you mean?"

"I think about the spirit of the ancient Liburnians, the people who lived in prehistoric times in the country where I come from. This spirit was carried so proudly by Mihovil, the spirit of the warrior and visionary who emerged from the harsh island environment that forced these ancient people not only to comply with the Laws of Nature, but to become masters of them."

"Like the magic powers that many ancient people have mastered?"

"Yes. My grandmother Lucija, a woman keeper of an archaic tradition of mantra chanting, left me a record of them. Before I went to Lebanon when I was still in Croatia, I found my grandmother's book. In the book were preserved mantras and magic formulas by which divine powers had been invoked. In quest of the original script of the ancient Croatians, Mihovil most likely went towards the ancient Levant from where, according to the legend, early Liburnians, our ancestors, arrived around the 12th and 11th centuries B.C. The island legends in the archaic Chakavian dialect that have been preserved in the northern Adriatic referred to these maritime migrations. They are the link to the Vedic linguistic heritage of Croatians."

"Antonija, I am here to help you. For the therapy to be successful it is important to accept the existence of a real person, your loved one. He is important for the outcome of therapy because of your feelings for him. In this way, you can overcome your fear of that other person who may be Mihovil's double or only a result of your imagination."

"I am connected to my Mihovil only by love. The feeling of unrest tells me that another part of him, under the guise of a ghost, has something secretly in mind for me."

"Visualize mentally the image of your Mihovil and then let it go slowly. After that we can start with the *Indigo Color Therapy*. I think you are ready."

"What do I have to do?"

"It would be helpful for you to focus your attention

on your *Third Eye* or *Indigo Chakra* between your eyebrows. Focusing your attention there and visualizing the indigo color, you will dive into the spiral etheric whirlpools and connect to the finer powers. The indigo color can help you alleviate the condition of melancholia and transcend it. In that way you can clear the way for the appearance of your loved one."

And so indeed it was. By the power of the spirit, I soon freed myself from the condition of melancholia, the outcome of which could have had far-reaching consequences. Returning to a more balanced mindset, I not only achieved a harmonious resonance of the whole body, but also felt completely in tune with the vibrations of Nature.

The response came not long after. It was an early Saturday morning in May when at the door of my hotel room I found a bunch of fragrant lilies.

LONG AWAITED ENCOUNTER

The city was glittering in moonlight that was shimmering into the windows of the skyscrapers. A ray of a silvery light was shining through my windows, touching me gently. I moved away from the window and took off a silver scarf that was wrapped around my shoulders. I was about to go into the room when I heard a soft rustle at the windows. I shivered. I heard another rustle; then I felt a kiss on my shoulder and a breath that was alluring like the scent of lily.

I turned around. Mihovil was standing in front of me. He looked more beautiful than ever. He was gazing at me with his translucent black eyes full of tears. The blue-green bow-tie, negligently stuck in a white collar that was jutting out of the elegant suit jacket of the same color, accentuated their beauty. He approached me. He started talking in a quiet, gentle voice, "Antonija!"

"Mihovil, my love, is that you?"

"Come closer," I heard a soft voice.

I couldn't resist. I approached stretching my hands out to the figure, illuminated by an invisible source of light. As soon as I tried to touch him, he would lose his shape. He didn't have a physical body.

"Mihovil?"

"My dear, Antonija."

"I don't see you; I can only feel you."

"Antonija, it is me. I am out of my body. I can't be like this much longer. You called me, and asked for the path that leads to my soul. I came to tell you that you can always call me if you open your heart. Nothing else but true love could bring you closer to me."

"Mihovil!" I stretched my hands to him surrounded by opaque darkness. I discerned the blurred contour. I entered the high field of an invisible aura. The closer I got, the more heat I could feel. It was spreading like the small tongues of a flame from open lily petals at the base of my feet. I was out of my body. I realized that when I tried to touch the saucy, lily flower with the tips of my fingers. Kissing the place where the Mihovil's eyelids appeared in the outline, I saw a purple flame blazing out of the luminous petals.

While I was merging with Mihovil embraced by light, I could feel the waves of energy climbing along my spinal column up to the top of my head. We began our dance. We were swaying in the ecstatic ritual, with the rhythm of accelerating spasms. Then faster and faster, as though we were exceeding the limits of our own being until we were united in the light. Then a hush fell. The sway stopped in the blink of an eye. Carried by the dance of this flared up passion, I returned slowly back into my body. In the place where Mihovil had been standing, I could discern only an indistinct aura. His figure was gradually fading away, leaving sparkles, mottled with the golden circles that were spreading around him sending to me the energy of love. I tried to call him. He didn't respond. Before he faded completely away, the words appeared in my mind, *It is as though the Goddess Anzotika herself descended from heaven gifting us with this encounter and bathing us in the eternal light on whose waves we danced our dance of love.*

AN UNINVITED GUEST

I let my mind float away into the embrace of night. I let my hair down and began taking off my clothes. After I took off the last piece of clothing, I slipped into the warm bed. I tried to fall asleep, but sleep wouldn't come. It wouldn't even come with my silent mantra, nor with the rhythm of the song that was coming from a distance that reminded me of the gentle whispering of the lovers.

I uncovered myself, lifting the plush blanket. I placed my hand on my soft breast. Then I felt a touch, a cold touch without feeling. There was Mihovil's double standing in front of me almost with the same appearance and the same blue-green bow-tie negligently stuck in a white collar. I was startled by his look, the arrow in his deep black eye that had pierced my heart. Fear gripped me, and then I felt a sudden flicker in my heart. It started fluttering with a blissful energy, enthralled by the ardor of love. I just wanted to be, to share the joy of love.

The faceless figure was disappearing from my sight. His malicious laughter was followed by a speech without passion, "Was the young lady content with the hospitality? Did she enjoy the pastry?"

I wanted to shout when I got a mild hit in the temple. I fell into bed. I could distinguish the words, "I'll get you yet!"

The last thing that I remembered before I lost consciousness was a curtain swaying gently in the wind, shielding the barely visible figure. I could hear the steps of the passersby in the distance accompanied by the rattle of the window that the visitor had left open.

TOMORROW MORNING, BEFORE THE first patient appeared in my office, the phone that Khalil gave me rang. As though he felt intuitively that something was going on, he wanted to hear my voice. Hearing his warm voice, I instantly regained a cheerful spirit, "Antonija, I had to call you. How are you doing?"

"I am happy with my job. My colleagues are trustworthy. I could confide in them not only in business matters but in personal as well. However, in private matters, nothing is working out in my favor. I wanted so much for Mihovil to be close to me. I was invoking him by my body and my soul. One night he finally came. I think that his appearance is mysteriously connected with the object of the triangle pyramid structure. It belonged to the eccentric Gypsy woman from Jerusalem who prophesied the end of the world. After I returned from the opera, I stared at the object. Then the encounter with Mihovil happened. And after that, a frightening encounter with his double. I don't know if I can withstand our next encounter."

"Antonija, put the object away somewhere and don't stare at it anymore. The most important thing is that you managed to keep your presence of mind," Khalil said firmly.

"Not only do my Liburnian Goddesses protect me, but you are always here when I need you."

"Yes, I am by your side, just as your Liburnian Goddesses: We will always be by your side. However, be careful. You can't imagine what is going on around you."

"I can guess, Khalil. There is something I didn't tell you. Not so long ago some agents were sneaking around my office. They threatened to kill me if I didn't tell them Mihovil's whereabouts."

"Why didn't you tell me, Antonija? They were certainly not my agents."

"I don't understand, Khalil."

"It's not the right time now, Antonija. I owe you an explanation. I'll explain everything to you at some other time. I have to go now. Take care. Anyway, you shouldn't invoke Mihovil anymore."

"It was part of the therapy. But it will be as you wish, my dear friend. I'll try to restrain myself."

"Everything will be fine. However, be ready for anything."

"For sure, Khalil, I know. I am ready."

"Don't worry, you will always be protected by the Goddesses and your earthly friend," Khalil said with confidence and hung up the phone.

GETTING READY
FOR THE
CONFERENCE

The happy news about the conference on Clinical Medical Anthropology which was supposed to be held in cooperation with the Medical Center of Columbia University[89] at the end of September, came with a breath of fresh air during an early morning in June.

I entered my office and opened the window widely, admiring the majestic scenery of a rainbow hanging over the river. The smile of the glittering rainbow that was rising in a ring elicited the same feeling in the sleepy passersby, waking them up.

I sat, pensive in my chair, searching through my papers for the conference report template. I knew I

---

[89] Columbia University Medical Center traces its roots to 1767 when Dr. Samuel Bard founded the medical department of King's College, which later became the College of Physicians and Surgeons at Columbia University.

must have left it with the other important papers on my desk. I thought I misplaced it somewhere, but after lunch, Elza informed me that she had them. "Antonija, my apologies. I took the liberty to look through your papers because I needed the conference report template urgently. I hope you don't mind."

"Quite the contrary."

"Your work is impressive. It's remarkable how you explain the variability of symptoms of different medical and psychiatric illnesses regarding various cultural affiliations. The center of your attention is on the archaic culture of southeastern Europe which is particularly informative."

"If we consider illness as a cultural phenomenon, we can see how the different cultures deal with illness in different ways. So-called 'primitive cultures', to which we can add the culture of the ancient Liburnians including the one that my Mihovil studied, employ magical patterns to understand and explain disease. What I am mostly interested in is how the shamans used to heal, who quite likely were women of ancient Liburnia. We can assume that like ancient shamans in the ecstatic cult, they called on the spirits of their ancestors and their mythical world to reach for another plane of existence in order to achieve personal integrity and to be healed. I just wanted to follow in Mihovil's footsteps. That's why I chose this theme."

"Nice."

Elza looked at me while sipping a coffee.

"The whole summer is in front of us. I am sure you will prepare in a scholarly manner for the autumn conference. Maybe Ellen and Michael can help you. May I ask them?"

"Sure, I'll be glad to."

"They will get in touch with you after the lunch break. Be in your room."

"I will be there."

Elza laid the tray aside. She put on a light linen scarf and went to the door. She said from the threshold, "I forgot the most important thing. Don't tire yourself. Take it easy Antonija."

Elza's words kept ringing in my ears while I was walking up the corridor to my office. I went towards the window where I used to find moments of peace. I was watching a sailing boat of an unusual shape moving across the Hudson River. Its tall sails stretched to the top of the mast. I imagined the sails silently fluttering in the wind. The scenery reminded me of a feeling of wonder and peace, taking me for instance back to my hometown of Preko. Tears came to my eyes while my mind was drifting, sailing across the river. I recoiled at the sound of the door handle. I quickly collected myself when I heard Ellen and Michael talking lively, "First of all, we have to contact the World Health Organization and gather the statistical information about the prevalence rates of the psychosomatic disorders in the general population."

"Are you saying that I will gather the information, but you will write the work and sign it? Is that what you wanted to tell me?" Ellen acrimoniously opposed Michael's plan.

"Calm down, dear young people. We will sign it together," I said, trying to alleviate the tense atmosphere.

"In reverence, Dr. Antonija," Michael turned to me.

"Thank you," added Ellen.

"Forget about the statistical data. Here is the conference report template."

Michael leaned towards the text that I prepared this morning. He read the title in disbelief, "Magical cultural patterns in treatment of disease in the archaic cultures of southeastern Europe." He put the paper aside and gave me a perplexed look, "How can I be of assistance? I have no clear idea about what the southeastern Europe culture represents."

"As I read in your resume, you have a good

knowledge of the history of the North American Indians. It won't be hard for you to draw a parallel between the nations, as we know that the same consciousness archetypes could be found in all the nations and cultures of the world. They share a similar mythological code in their stories and their mythical traditions. They go deeply into the prehistoric mythical world explaining life, death and beyond and the relationship between man and the Universe in a similar way."

"Well, interesting. I haven't thought about that connection."

"Here are the materials. You will have something to study during the summer." I handed Michael a pile of papers, organized in folders in chronological order. "These are my notes from different world conferences."

"You are an excellent scientist, Dr. Antonija. It will be my honor to work with you," Michael said. He seemed to be feeling more cheerful.

"I will be at your disposal," Ellen joined in.

"Thank you. I would like to be alone for a while," I said and walked the visitors to the door. I returned to the window to take a break. I gazed into the distance and again saw the sailing boat. It sailed away in the direction of the United Nations building.

AT COLUMBIA
UNIVERSITY

The autumn was approaching at a leisurely pace. Among its colorful heralds the most prominent were violet china asters. Their vivid tones were lively, contrasting with the gentle tones of lilies. You could find them everywhere. They adorned the window-sills in my office. Their petals displayed vivid, violet-bluish skyglow.

Dusk was falling. Lights were lighting up quietly in the distance. I was thinking about my time spent abroad. I hoped that the conference report that I had to present together with Ellen and Michael the next morning at Columbia University was the last report in the sabbatical year, after which I looked forward to returning home.

It was a rare coincidence that at the same time as our medical conference, the Iranian President delivered a speech at Columbia University. Elza drew my attention to it at the last moment while I was already on my way to the university. After a brief argument, she finally agreed to let me go to listen to the speaker. It was, after all, an opportunity for Ellen and Michael to present the report in my absence. According to competent reviewers, the report threw new light on the current anthropological inquiries into the archaic cultures of southeastern Europe, with special reference to the culture of the ancient Liburnians. Liburnian culture could be traced back to the primeval Indo-European mythology that permeates the mythical stories and legends preserved on the northern Adriatic islands that are possibly the link to the Vedic linguistic heritage of the proto-Croatians.

When I entered the hall, the incomprehensible prayers were reverberating through it. I assumed that they came from the Holy Quran. They were uttered by the main guest, the Iranian President, who seemed to be speaking to the audience on behalf of God. There was an uproar after the first words he uttered. It was a clear sign that his speech would not be delivered without political provocations. Not interested in the speaker's message, I kept my eye on his smug smile that was flickering upon his lips. Then I fixed my gaze on his dull gray suit that was in tune with his insignificant-looking figure. He was a great speaker. He managed to disguise his fanatical ideas with deliberately patronizing religious and philosophical messages.

Nothing that I heard this morning aroused my attention. Except, maybe, one detail regarding the President's well-known Holocaust denial. I recalled the comment of a renowned journalist on the deep historical roots of the Israeli-Iranian confrontation that I read somewhere. They were recorded in the Old Testament in the Book of Esther where Haman, the chief minister of the Persian king Ahasuerus[90], decided to exterminate the Jews throughout the whole kingdom. The Iranian President was, according to the journalist's comment, a reincarnation of a Persian Haman. That's why I wasn't surprised by the President's point of view.

A strong handshake interrupted my thoughts. Then I smelled a delicate fragrance of perfume, that I recognized instantly. I stood up to hug Khalil, but he stopped me suddenly. He took my hand. We left before the commotion started of the audience giving the speaker a send-off applause and a malicious smile here and there.

---

[90] Ahasuerus (Greek Xerxes), a Persian king, ruled 485-465 B.C. He was mentioned in the Book of Esther in the Old Testament. Xerxes, the First was most likely the Persian king identified as Ahasuerus. (Esth 3:6).

KHALIL TOOK ME TO the hotel. To my surprise, he stayed at the same hotel as I and chose a room next to mine. When we entered the hotel, I understood why.

"Antonija, I couldn't talk about it at the conference," Khalil turned to me. I caught his piercing look that hinted that I shouldn't ask him anything. I suppressed the question as to why he suddenly appeared without saying hello. He grabbed the cellphone that I had been using. When he opened it, it was more than obvious why he had given it to me. Beneath its digital face lay a .22-caliber gun capable of firing several bullets swiftly.

"Antonija, tomorrow is the opening of the main debate of the 62nd Session of the General Assembly of the United Nations[91]. There are all the indications that something is going to happen. Please, be sure to have your phone with you."

"I will."

"If you need something, you know you can call. I have to go now. If everything goes as planned, I'll knock on your door in the morning. If I don't come before eight o'clock, go by yourself to the United Nations building. Here is a special pass. They won't check you."

[91] The 62nd Session of the General Assembly of the United Nations was held from September 18th to December 22nd 2007.

"Are you sure?"

"The pass guarantees you diplomatic immunity. Take the cellphone and wait for my call," Khalil said firmly and hurried towards the door.

AT THE 62ND SESSION OF THE GENERAL ASSEMBLY OF THE UNITED NATIONS

The dawn was breaking with the rosy colors of the distant sky rising above the highest rooftops. The clock hand struck six o'clock. In less than five minutes I heard the knock on the door. I thought that it must have been Khalil who had arrived earlier than expected. I ran towards the door half-covered by a blanket. I froze, staring at the waiter with the morning delivery. I took the tray full of fresh food. I put it on the little serving table and opened the white envelope with the United Nations monogram. It was an official invitation card. I didn't pay much attention to it. I was more concerned that Khalil hadn't come. I got dressed quickly. I grabbed a full-dress suit from the hanger. I put on high heels. I summoned up my courage and ran towards the United Nations building.

I arrived just when the Secretary-General of the United Nations was delivering his welcoming speech. I sat on a seat in the middle of the hall with a nice view as no one was blocking it. The speakers were talking one after another. After the last speaker delivered his speech in the morning part of the program, I went to have a snack at the official restaurant. I walked through the rigorous checkpoint with my special pass. I held my purse firmly shielding it with my hand from curious eyes.

I was hungry since I had missed breakfast. I ate more than usual – a crispy, coconut pastry for dessert. When I bit into the last small piece, I glanced at a man at the last table in the row in front of me. He seemed familiar, and I wasn't surprised when he smiled, signaling me to come closer.

I understood that he wanted to tell me something. I winced as I saw Khalil running towards the exit on the opposite side. I had the feeling that the agent who had attacked me in my office looking for Mihovil was also there. The cocked hat exposed him. He obviously wore it as an identification sign. I thought he was here for the same reason as I. Soon he disappeared from my sight. I approached a man whose appearance reminded me of the Israeli Rabbi. He stretched his mouth into a cordial smile revealing a line of pure white teeth with

pleasant-smelling breath. He started speaking loudly
so everybody could hear, showing his pleasure at seeing me again. I finally recognized Jerusalem's Rabbi
Yitzhak, the old Rabbi with notably wilted cheeks. I
fell into his embrace letting him kiss me. When he
then kissed my hand, he murmured that I sit on a seat
in the last row of the hall and wait for Khalil's call.

I entered the hall and sat on a middle seat in the
last row. I was waiting patiently hoping to see Khalil
while several speakers took their turns. When the
Iranian President appeared at the speaker's stand, I
pricked up my ears knowing I could expect anything.
However, I didn't expect that his speech would spark
protests and prompt delegations from several countries
to walk out of the assembly.

While the speaker's words were reverberating
through the hall with an imperative demand for the
world to divert from the path of the Devil, one detail
caught my attention. It seemed to me that for the second time he was talking to the audience in the name
of God. I had barely noticed how his figure perfectly
depicted the figure of the false prophet until on the
screen above the speaker's stand appeared the face of
the real prophet. I held my breath, putting a handker-
chief over my mouth. The audience raised a great out-
cry. The guests started to rise pointing their fingers at

the screen. Then I heard Khalil's cellphone. He asked me to go towards the back exit where he would be waiting. He said he suspected he knew where the prophet had gone and we should hurry so as not to lose him.

When I came to the back exit, Khalil signaled for me to follow him. He seemed not to know which direction to take. After a short reflection, he turned right. We were running for about twenty minutes. We stopped at the end of a long corridor in front of a room with a slightly opened door. I heard the noise of confused voices. The room was most likely behind the wall of the main speaker's stand.

Stepping into the room was like stepping into another time. The dead calm air enveloped me like an unearthly mist. It fell heavily on my shoulders and I felt powerless. I was standing absent-minded like a stone. Then I felt someone near me and a touch on my shoulders. I could tell who it was by the cold hand. My shoulders were trembling with fear, but I found the strength to raise my head. I pointed my finger at the prophet's eyes. His gaze seemed to be coming from the depths of the void. His cold, black eye was staring at me dully, piercing my eyelids. I tried to resist hitting him with my hand on his loins. I wondered how this monster could have appeared in the United Nations building. I tried to wrench myself free of the attacker's grip and open my purse. But he was faster. He put his arm about my waist and clasped me to his bosom. Just after disgust overwhelmed me, my fear subsided. Everything happened in a second, and I almost forgot about Khalil. I heard him shouting at the attacker to let me go. Somehow I managed to release my hand from the attacker's grasp. I pointed my finger again at his eyes in order to overpower him. His gaze made me feel dizzy. I almost fainted when I heard a shot. Khalil began to shoot while shouting at the attacker to let me go. He released me finally at the second shot. I thought that Khalil had shot the attacker in the leg, but he had only grazed him. After the third shot, the attacker moved towards the wall in the middle of the room. Then he went through the wall behind the picture of the American President. When we moved the picture, we found a secret passage to the next room into which the attacker mysteriously disappeared.

It felt as though a veil woven of the darkest darkness fell off my eyes. I collected my thoughts. I went closer to a table with the three chairs. There was a book on the table. The chair with its tall back resembled the presidential loggia at the theater. I touched the silky cover of the chair with my fingertips. It was still warm as though someone had just left. Khalil's stunned look indicated that it was someone totally unexpected. I approached Khalil and took the book. I was confused looking at the illegible signature at the bottom of the page. There was a space below left for the signature of the Secretary-General.

"Whose signature could it be?" I asked Khalil. He brought the book closer to his face and said, "I can discern the letters. You wouldn't believe it, Antonija! It's our prophet's signature!"

I looked closer. The letters flickered before my eyes. I turned to Khalil, with a sigh, "Yes, this is Ishmael's signature. Why his?" I looked at Khalil questioningly.

"There is some strange link between him and the shadow government, a unique World Government whose establishment would be supervised by the United Nations. We shall clarify it," Khalil said.

"Yes, I remember. His name was mentioned in that context during the intelligence gathering process when you scanned the voice of an employee at the Diplomatic Mission of Israel on the East River," I turned to Khalil noticing the grimace on his face. I paused for a moment and continued after some thought. "Wait, Khalil," I said looking away in hope to find anything that could dispel our doubts.

I took the book and started leafing through it. Before I came to the end, a sentence with an unintelligible content followed by numbers drew my attention.

"Khalil, come closer. Do you see what I see?" I said in disbelief.

Khalil opened the book to the next to the last page. It ended with September 18th, 2007. He looked at me and said worriedly, "Oh, my God! It's today! The Secretary-General's signature is missing. There are only a few hours left." Khalil sighed and pensively turned to me, "Who was the last speaker?"

"The Iranian President."

"Of course, the Iranian President. I am afraid he was used to divert the audience's attention. The agreement was signed when all the eyes of the world were focused on this clown."

"You and your agents! Couldn't you have prevented it from happening?" I asked Khalil sternly.

"Antonija, that couldn't prevent those more powerful from signing it either."

"I don't understand," I looked at Khalil questioningly.

"Antonija, it's time for you to know. Accept my agents as a *celestial police* working for the *Great Brotherhood of Light*. They are our ascended brothers in the higher realms of divine existence. We are all working for the well-being of humanity. You are one of us. And your Mihovil as well. Although I am not sure anymore about him. We shall find out if he is really Mihovil. What confuses me is that other one who looks completely like him."

"Ishmael?"

"Yes, Ishmael."

"How would we know who is the real one?"

"The real one is the one who has the genuine powers."

"What about Ishmael? Haven't people witnessed his demonstration of powers?" I shouted in disbelief.

"His powers are fake. They are not from the divine source," Khalil continued persuasively. "We have to hurry up. There is not much time left. We can still stop the Secretary-General from signing the agreement. It won't happen because YOU are going to stop it from happening!"

"I?" I looked at Khalil in astonishment.

"Yes, you Antonija. Wasn't it thanks to you that the new king whose coming was recently heralded by Ishmael was thwarted from sitting in the Temple of Jerusalem?"

"Thanks to the higher powers of my Liburnian Goddesses," I said to Khalil, recalling the being with deep-set, translucent, black, hypnotic eyes. I pulled myself together hearing Khalil, "Let me take care of the Secretary-General. Go back to Croatia. In Croatia you can find the answer to Mihovil's disappearance."

"Back to Croatia? How many days have I been dreaming about it?" I approached Khalil and kissed him on his forehead. "Well, are you going to tell Elza? I couldn't disappoint her now after she won an honorable mention with our conference report at Columbia University."

"Don't worry. Pack up. We are flying to Frankfurt together tomorrow. I have something to do there."

"Yes, Khalil," I said readily, "the only thing we have to think about is how to get out of the United Nations building unnoticed."

"That's the least of our worries," he said with confidence, and then dialed a number on his cellphone. After a while a man in a security guard suit appeared. I gave him a wink, recognizing Rabbi Yitzhak.

THE
LEGEND
OF
KORNATI

V

UPON MY RETURN
TO CROATIA

Listening to the song of the crickets, I let myself fall contentedly into the embrace of night. I was drifting off into a sleep that was off and on disrupted by the deluge of agitated waves and the screams of the seagulls. I fell asleep thinking of how successfully I had overcome all the obstacles and had returned from abroad feeling content.

I spent the first days in Preko. I didn't want to call anybody. I was yearning for solitude. A desolate place in the early autumn was an ideal place to collect myself. However, not even the power of the primordial beauty that was energizing every atom of my being could overcome the dreary thought coming from my subconscious and flowing forward with numerous questions about where to look for Mihovil.

Coming back from the store with the newspaper one morning, I stared at the front page. As though I had wandered into an ancient time, words with dramatic content appeared before my eyes: "Will Jerusalem return to a peace that it hadn't experienced since 970 B.C. when King Solomon reigned for forty years?" The text was followed by an unrecognizable surreal image of Jerusalem with heaven opened wide above the city and the doors where the evil black eye appeared. I tried not to pay attention to it, but I was caught up in its magic spell. I was absorbed into it in the twinkling of an eye and found myself in front of the walls of Jerusalem.

The Old City welcomed me in a new guise. Instead of the apocalyptic reality that I was expecting, the atmosphere was filled with such a perfect peace that I wondered where I was. When I approached the temple that was rising on the site of the Mosque of Omar, I realized that it wasn't the Jerusalem that I had left behind.

The new temple had a triangular-pyramidal shape, the same as the pendant on the eccentric Gypsy woman's necklace. A sense of celestial peace came over me as I visualized it. You could have felt the peace everywhere. Approaching the temple, there was a big stone board with a carved scepter and a handhold in the form of a crystal black eye on the right side. I came closer. Then I saw the figure of a young man behind it. He floated out of a mist that surrounded him. He approached me and addressed me in an indifferent tone. His monotonous voice didn't reveal any feelings. He told me what I already knew from the article in the newspaper about the latest developments in this part of the world: In the countries of the Middle East there was a new feeling of peace and prosperity after a beloved leader came to power. *The Antichrist?* It crossed my mind, *but who is this young man? Mihovil? Ishmael?* During my inner monologue, the young man's face started to change. His eyebrow above the left eye raised and a slightly crossed eye started rotating. The perspective changed. As though he came out of the newspaper itself, the young man was suddenly in my arms. His face appeared more mature, his bearing more dignified. He had a full-dress suit and a big diamond ring on his ring finger.

I held my fiancé's hand. We were stepping to the altar. We stopped at the strong stroke of a gong. The timeless chords started reverberating. The black diamond eye, studded with multicolored crystals appeared above the altar. The same eye was glittering on my fiancé's hand. Enthralled by its glitter, I was listening unquestioningly to the words that were coming from the tall altar, "What God has joined together, let not the Promised Son separate." The diamond rain began to pour. It sprinkled me when my fiancé handed me the ring. He approached me and took the laced veil off my face. I was standing like a stone when I saw the floating figure of the Goddess Anzotika in front of me. At the moment that my fiancé wanted to kiss me, Anzotika's resolute voice filled the atmosphere, "Antonija, you mustn't surrender to him. He is not your real fiancé. Just listen to your heart: Find a place for true love in it and your Divine Fiancé will come."

I dropped the newspaper. I was staring motionless at the empty newspaper page. The scent of the fresh sea air was drifting through the slightly open window. It was slowly filling my nostrils bringing strength to my body. I knew that the answer to the question of who my real fiancé was could only be found in my homeland.

I WENT BY THE late ferry-boat to Zadar. I decided to call Alka as soon as I arrived. I put my luggage down. I slowly went towards the phone thinking about what to tell her. I hoped she wouldn't be angry that I hadn't called her during the last year. When I heard her cheerful voice, I instantly let go of my discomfort, "Antonija, I was thinking so much of you. If you hadn't called, I would have called you myself. I have almost finished working on the book. There are only a few pages left."

"Amazing! How wonderful that you welcome me with such nice news!"

"Your return is a most beautiful gift to me!" Alka said excitedly asking me to come to see her immediately. I asked her to have patience. I postponed the meeting until the beginning of the next week. I wanted to call Dr. Sandalic first of all to tell him about the insights Khalil's *celestial police* had gained.

WITH DR. SANDALIC ON THE KORNATI ISLANDS[92]

I was in a hurry in the early morning to get to the meeting with Dr. Sandalic. We met at our old meeting place, his office at the Faculty of Philosophy. I arrived breathless fifteen minutes late. The good-natured professor smiled at me and gave me a gentlemanly compliment, saying that I had become prettier while being abroad. My keen eye noticed a vague unrest in the quivering smile on his lips. His anxiety was also obvious from the way he approached me as he delivered his friend's news about Mihovil's possible whereabouts.

"Antonija, by a series of mysterious circumstances, the secret police became interested in Mihovil. It was my fault, excuse me."

[92] The Kornati Islands are an archipelago consisting of 140 islands, the largest and densest archipelago in the Adriatic Sea.

"I don't understand," I responded with a confused look on my face.

"As you probably remember, I advised you to do a forensic analysis to determine the age of the text of the book. I confided in my colleague, an expert in forensic archeology and criminology. He spread the story about the significant discovery. It didn't take too long for the news to spread. I heard a rumor that the secret police searched for Mihovil. Interestingly, I haven't had any news for a long time until now when I just got a call from my source and you miraculously appear in the doorway."

"Where is Mihovil?" I uttered excitedly.

"I cannot say for sure as I don't have tangible evidence. However, the information that I just got from the high-ranking police officer might be helpful. As far as he knew, last summer a man was spotted of similar appearance in front of a small fisherman's cottage in one of the secluded coves of the Kornati Islands."

"Why didn't he tell you earlier?"

"My colleague made a glancing reference to it. I didn't want to disregard the information, as I thought it might be of some help."

"Do you know where the place is?"

"I'll have the photo in about an hour."

"I'll go home to pick up a few things. I'll be in front of the faculty building in exactly one hour."

"Antonija, what do you have in mind?"

"I am going with you to the Kornati Islands."

"Well, I cannot argue with that. I promised you I would look for Mihovil!" he answered resonantly and, as a true gentleman, was here for me in perhaps the most important moment of my life.

"Thank you, see you later," I answered, feeling very relieved as I went to the door.

When I came back, I didn't have to wait long for Dr. Sandalic. While I was parking, he appeared in the front of the faculty building. He waved me towards his car. Seeing the well kept, safe old Volvo, I joined him immediately.

"Here is a photo," Dr. Sandalic said as he turned to me, taking a colorful photo out of his pocket. Then he started the engine and turned the radio on. The old evergreen songs began to play. I was holding the photo, my thoughts drifting to the secluded cove of the Kornati Islands that graced the small fisherman's village like a jewel. Dr. Sandalic interrupted my train of thought.

"In half an hour we are departing by my sailboat from the marina Borik. Be ready, we might spend the night."

"I'll stay as long as necessary," I said without hesitation and asked curiously, "who will navigate?"

"I am your driver and your protector, don't worry," he said confidently.

"I don't doubt that you will do a good job," I responded and looked outside the car. Leaving behind the city outline, my thoughts were wandering far away towards our destination. I jolted at Dr. Sandalic's voice, "Here we are, Antonija."

I got out of the car and headed towards Dr. Sandalic and the lonely sailboat that was docked near the beacon. It looked like an aged beauty with its bow swinging in the breeze. I stepped on the deck and stashed my backpack with a few personal items. Dr. Sandalic joined me soon after he released the berth and raised the anchor. He started the engine and headed out with the unfurled sails toward the Island of Ugljan.

I went to the bow. I sat on the straw mat, wanting to catch some sun before it descended behind the horizon. Dr. Sandalic nodded to me without uttering a word. He didn't seem to be interested in conversation. He took the role of a silent participant of a journey with an uncertain ending. I didn't want to disturb him. I closed my eyes feeling the caress of the gentle breeze as I listened to the breaking waves striking the boat.

It was smooth sailing until we approached the Zdrelac Passage[93]. A strong wind suddenly began to gust and Dr. Sandalic quickly spread the mainsail and started sailing downwind toward the Dugi Otok[94]. He slowed down when approaching a narrow passage between the Dugi Otok and the Kornati Islands. Then, under full sail, he headed out again to the open sea. The view of so many Kornati outer islands was breathtaking. Even Dr. Sandalic uttered a word of praise, remembering what George Bernard Shaw said, "On the last day of Creation, God desired to crown his work and thus created the Kornati Islands out of tears, stars and breath." Enthralled, I turned to Dr. Sandalic with a benevolent smile. He returned it overcome by the beauty too.

The rest of the trip I spent admiring the hidden corners of nature in the secluded cove of the Donji Kornati Islands[95]. We were almost there. I was wondering why the hunters went to look for Mihovil in the backwoods of the islands. Observing island shapes and the cliffs with their edges that were going deep

---

[93] The Zdrelac Passage is the sea corridor between Ugljan and the neighboring Island of Pasman in the Zadar archipelago in the Adriatic Sea.

[94] Dugi Otok (Long Island) is the seventh largest island in the Adriatic Sea. It is a part of the Zadar archipelago.

[95] Donji Kornati, Cr. - Lower Kornati.

into the sea, I felt the whole scene was unearthly. Dr. Sandalic broke my reverie when he announced that we had reached our destination, the secluded fisherman's cottage on the barren, rocky cove I had seen in the colorful photo.

I got off the sailboat. While Dr. Sandalic was hanging around the berth adjusting the anchor, I went towards the old fisherman's cottage. Looking for the keys, I reached with my hand around the earthen pot by the entrance door, grabbing a clump of dirt. There were no keys to be found and the doors were closed. I was about to go to the back side of the house when Dr. Sandalic caught up with me. I had a vague sense of foreboding. My soul trembled. Dr. Sandalic carefully made one hesitant step forward with me following. After the third step, he coura-geously went around the corner. I then ran towards the back of the house. An unbearable smell, mixed with the smell of the sun-drenched macchia bush filled my nostrils.

There was a barely recognizable, decomposed body lying on the ground. The crystal clear slightly crossed black eye was miraculously preserved. It was staring at me from the massacred face. I was standing help-less in a lonely, gloomy spot believing it was the face of Ishmael. I almost lost consciousness when I felt a small, flickering hope in my soul which gave me faith that I would meet Mihovil again.

I hesitantly approached the lifeless body. I wanted to touch it, but Dr. Sandalic stopped me. He said suddenly, "Antonija, we shouldn't touch anything. I'll call my friend the police officer. He'll send a patrol. The way the body was massacred I would say it was done by well-established interrogation methods. Only forensics could determine if it was the body of your Mihovil. We shall wait for the results."

I refused to believe he wasn't here anymore. I wished with every bone in my body for him to be alive. My woman's intuition had its own reasons to believe it strongly.

I looked at Dr. Sandalic. He must have guessed something, although he most likely didn't know about Ishmael. Not thinking much I thought it was better to leave it like that. I nodded tacitly and then went back to the boat. It was almost dark. I went to my cabin fraught with sadness. I fell on the bed. I let my imagination get the best of me. In the glittering eyes of the night boiling with passion, I saw Mihovil's figure. Catching the tears from the stars that were sprinkling in the sighs of love, I drifted off into sleep with gentle thoughts.

Around dawn I heard Dr. Sandalic talking to someone. I again fell asleep firmly believing that the body found wasn't the body of my Mihovil.

THE ANSWER TO THE MYSTERY ABOUT THE BOOK OF GRANDMOTHER LUCIJA

Returning to Zadar it took me some time to come to my senses. I rallied my strength and went to the Municipal Loggia to look for Alka. As I guessed, she was sitting in a deep, contemplative pose staring into the space in front of her. She jolted at the creak of the door and closed the book.

"Alka, it's me!" I exclaimed and ran towards Alka.

Once she became aware of my presence, she jumped for joy and said cheerfully, "Antonija, you came at the right time. The mystery of the book is solved."

I looked at Alka in disbelief. She took my hand and sat me at the table by the book. She lit the candle and started moving it lightly over the back of the page until some text appeared. The new words were slowly forming from letters and a sentence from the words. I opened my mouth to speak, but Alka suddenly interrupted me. She turned to me and said solemnly, "The last woman warrior of the Liburnians will save her people!" These were the last words of the book.

"Congratulations, Alka, my dearest sorceress!"

Alka looked straight through me as if I wasn't there. She came to my attention when I asked her about the last time she saw the librarian Milica. She wondered why I asked her that. She said she didn't remember, but she heard she was fired for some mysterious reason. I asked her how to get in touch with Milica. She gave me her address as she didn't have her phone. I went to the door. I kissed Alka on the cheek and asked her to keep silent about everything. Her firm handshake at the door told me that she understood everything I said. I hurried to the car, leaving the building. Then I went toward Borik.

It was already dark when I came to the last house in the row. It was hidden by tall palm trees. Constantly looking over my shoulder, I went cautiously forward. I boldly rang the doorbell. The door opened only after the third ring. I wasn't expecting to see a pale-faced, miserable figure with bloated cheeks. Looking at this once pretty, charming woman I felt pity.

"Come in, Dr. Antonija."

We went into the living room. The disorganized room was a reflection of an unstable, very sick person.

"Oh my God!" I exclaimed.

"I apologize for the mess, Dr. Antonija. Please have a seat!"

I sat on an upholstered bench with lacquered handholds which showed that she had once been a noble woman. I coughed and then asked her straightforward, "Milica, did you give someone a book?"

She began to stammer. I encouraged her to continue. She relaxed after I told her several times that I didn't represent anyone's interest and that there was nothing to fear.

"That morning I went to check if everything was in place in the room. I noticed from the door that the cabinet with the book was unlocked. I found our Mihovil with his head buried in a book. I asked him if he would like to have some coffee. He stared daggers at me and my blood froze in my veins. He raised his hand pointing for me to leave. When I came back, he wasn't there anymore. There was the open book lying on the table. I think there was one page torn from the book. At its place was a note that I gave to you."

"Thank you, Milica. You have clarified a lot." I put my hand on her shoulder. I wanted to go to the door, but Milica stopped me.

"That's not all, Dr. Antonija. Since then I have had nightmares. The figure of our Mihovil has been constantly following me. In fact, two of them. I felt that I had lost my mind. I couldn't tell anyone. I believed I was getting crazier and crazier. I thought the only way out was to take my life. And then you appeared. Maybe God Himself sent you to me."

"Everything is all right, dear Milica. There is nothing to fear," I answered warmly and shook her hand. "We are going to resolve your condition. You will be under my therapy until you return to work."

"Thank you, Dr. Antonija."

"I have to go now. I have something to do. But I'll come by to see you at the first opportunity."

I hugged this slightly built woman with a very perplexed look on her face. Then she grabbed my hand tightly not wanting to let go and with trembling steps walked me to the door.

IN THE NAGA KINGDOM

I arrived late at my apartment. I went to the bathroom, took a shower, and went to the bedroom. I put a silk kimono on, something I always do before starting meditation. I did it instinctively, wanting to clarify the last remaining issue about what really happened to Mihovil that had been bothering me since the very beginning. I turned the light off. Then I took the beads out of my pocket and started chanting the mantra. Thoughts were coming in sequences. When they disappeared, usually misty bluish-violet light appeared as I went deep inside myself to find my true spiritual Self. But this time I felt tired and just fell into a deep sleep.

My dream brought me back to the past. I found myself by the rock cliff where I left Mihovil after the banquet at the Hotel President. I gave Mihovil my hand and he helped me walk down the rock cliff. I clumsily relied on my hand and the hem of my dress got snagged on the rock cliff. All of a sudden I felt dizzy and then I fainted. I tried to bend down to reach the hem of the dress when I saw a beautiful sea pearl. It shone in the seashell of an unusual shape that was standing untouched on the rock cliff. I stretched my hand to reach the pearl. A big wave suddenly arose and almost swallowed me. I stretched my hand a little further lightly touching the pearl. The moment after it transformed into a snake that pulled me down to the bottom of the sea.

I was carried by the beautiful giant purple fluorescent snake into a dark and endless void of space under the sea. She revealed herself as a protectress of the submarine world. The light was shining from her pearly, brilliant eyes illuminating the way to the sea bottom. It was so dark that I couldn't see anything. We were going deeper and deeper. I thought we were going to the beginning of creation and would not return.

It seemed to me that we finally arrived. The snake dropped me on the bottom of the seafloor. She said that according to legend that was being told in these lands, only a divine being could have touched the sea bottom to collect the golden dust of creation, to bring it to the surface and to breathe life into man.

I arrived at the endless Naga Kingdom. Residing there were the beings who sacrificed themselves to serve mankind eternally. They shined a light on the path of those on Earth who were ready to make a similar sacrifice. And indeed, a stunning light emerged from somewhere on the ocean floor, spreading all the way to the surface of the sea. The light was emerging from a strange organism right under my feet. It looked like a bluish-green gem plunged into the coral sand. It was obvious that it was a living organism, some kind of a lively intelligence that was emitting the light at certain intervals. The light resembled the fluorescent glow often seen by fishermen. This phenomenon was recorded by science fiction writers, but rarely reported by newspapers or magazines. It remained virtually unnoticed by most of the world. I decided that the intervals in which the light was emitted were most likely a coded message for a human being.

I took another step and lightly touched the sandy sea bed when something similar to a door opened. It was the entrance to an endless sub-sea cave. The further I went, the darker and darker it got. The surrounding flora consisted of gentle, whitish sea algae that were creating a mirror reflection in the space around them. The stunning image was amplified by the glow of small fireflies that resembled planktons dispersed in the surrounding space like the stars in the night sky. Further on, I came across numerous tiny passages that opened the moment I touched the

next rock cliff. Each one of them had their own magic
protectress: a sea siren. They all greeted me with deep
reverence telling me that I was one of the few who had
ever visited their kingdom.

I was floating in the space between the numerous passages. Then the snake turned to me and said
in a serious tone that caused me to turn ashen pale,
"Daughter, you came to us as you are the chosen one.
You are in the eternal, spirit kingdom, in between the
worlds. Only those who improved the well-being of
their own people with service and progressive ideas
can come to our kingdom."

Not believing what I heard, I asked the protectress
of the submarine world, "Am I alive?"

"Yes and no, depending on how you look at it. In
bodily form, in which you are now, you can be present
in different places at the same time. However, you
cannot retain this shape for much longer."

"In what shape am I now?"

"You are in ethereal shape now. More sensitive
people, the ones you call clairvoyants, can see it. They
are able to see different shapes. The seeing usually
occurs on the edge of reality and in a dream state.
You are now more a bisexual, androgynous being. You
are in this shape while you are with us in the spirit

world, but when you return to the people's world, you will transform back to the normal, human form. Only clairvoyants can recognize you in your present form."

I was tossing and turning while dreaming. I heard my voice calling Mihovil and spreading into the distance. The snake couldn't hear me. She stopped for an instant and then she took me deeper. She continued, "Come, we don't have much time left. I would like to show you the center of our kingdom. It's also the center of the world. Two paths diverge from it: the path of the light that leads to the east where divine beings can go in and out, and the path of darkness that leads to the west where the *shadows of evil* go in and out. This west path leads to the kingdom of our fallen brothers who fell from the path of good and swerved into the path of evil. It's the kingdom of darkness where dire serpentine beings reign. One of their branches left the Planet Earth and colonized other stars. It is better not to speak their names and to understand that they are the biggest threat to the Earth today."

I was struck dumb by these words. The snake paused and continued in a raised tone, "Now, the most important thing for you is to overpower Him!"

I cleared my thoughts. I remembered the coronation of the Devil. I recognized in his image the image of the Antichrist. I asked the snake, "I don't know where it was, but I recalled witnessing his coronation. Does it mean that he reigns somewhere?"

"Yes, in a precarious world where everything exists and yet does not exist at all. But the point is not his coronation. The point is that at this time his evil energy manifests itself through an individual, in this case, through the terrible being who is not of this world. What you have to prevent is that his energy and power don't take over the beautiful Earth. Because of the shift in space and time, it doesn't matter when you stop him. Whether in the past or in the future, you can always win. For as you win in one dimension, you win in all. You must defeat Him!" the snake said seriously.

"How?" I looked at her questioningly.

"By love. You can defeat Him only by love! You cannot lose!"

Yes, undoubtedly it is so, I said to myself. Remembering an important idea, I exclaimed excitedly, "His defeat will not mark the end, but the beginning of an era! A New era!"

"You are the herald of it," the snake uttered hissing. Then she pushed me with her tail, rushing me, "It's time to go. Before you get to the eastern door, you will go through a labyrinth through which I will send you with my eyes that will shine a light to show you the way."

Uttering this, the protectress of the submarine world transformed herself into a beautiful, graceful, and alluring Goddess. She took me to the hall which was the center of the world. There was nothing in the hall. It was made of pure gold. Not to disrupt the energy flow, we quickly flew to the eastern door. Then showing me the way out, my protectress said, "I'll know when you come. Come back to us as a winner!"

The heavy doors of the golden bars closed. I flew to the abyss, but saw no way out of it.

I was traveling through the vastness of the sea, moving through a labyrinth full of different kinds of beings, some of them human-like. The visibility was poor and I could barely discern their silhouettes. Approaching the spot that looked like a crossroads, I thought I saw a familiar glowing figure. I tried to swim towards him but was vigorously pulled by some force and raised to the sea surface.

MIHOVIL'S SHADOW

Feeling worn down, I was turning more and more to myself seeking refuge in my heart. I gradually started feeling better. However, neither by regular meditations nor by consistent daily routine, could I regain my strength and faith in myself. Khalil usually pulled me out of such a state of mind as though he felt telepathically that I needed him. He called when I least expected it, when I was in between several projects. To my surprise, once again in my time of need, he announced he was coming. He arrived one late Saturday afternoon by private jet from Beirut. He was well-dressed as usual. He wore a nice, sheer tailored suit that accentuated his dignified, almost noble bearing. He did not resemble an undercover policeman although he was one. I knew that he didn't arrive with good news as soon as I saw him.

"Antonija, a lot has happened since you returned to Croatia. Let's go to a place where we can be alone."

"Welcome, Khalil, regardless of the news you

have brought. Let's hurry to catch the last ferry-boat to Preko."

I took Khalil's baggage and put it in the trunk. Then I hurried towards the car-ferry landing. We arrived at the last minute before the ferry-boat left port with its loud horn blaring. Luckily, we were the only passengers and there was no reason to fear that anyone would see us. As soon as the ferry-boat landed, we quickly sneaked out and drove towards my house.

I noticed the mused expression on Khalil's face. Although he couldn't wait for me to prepare dinner, he started speaking immediately. He was drinking a cocktail. Then he turned to me.

"Antonija, we couldn't stop the Secretary-General from signing the agreement with Ishmael."

"Oh my God!" I exclaimed.

"That's not all," Khalil said looking for a piece of paper in his pocket. "Here is the report about the content of the text from the United Nations secret book. Cryptographers tried to analyze it in every possible way. The closest to the truth was a conclusion they came to that the leader, whomever he was, wanted to master the powers of the ancient Liburnians that you and Mihovil possess. He wanted to take your powers and become the ruler of Earth."

I wasn't surprised to hear these words. I remembered what the snake from the Naga Kingdom told me about the dire serpentine beings. They obviously lost their powers falling from the path of good and swerving into the path of evil. I turned to Khalil and said, "I don't understand how the Secretary-General could have signed the agreement."

"He must have thought it was the only way to save the Planet Earth. We all are aware that humanity is going towards its destruction."

"Yes, unfortunately we are," I responded. Then I took Khalil's hand and continued, "Khalil, I don't have better news either. Thinking that they killed Mihovil, the secret police agents most likely killed Ishmael. Mihovil, like his father, was in the way of those who opposed his research about the Non-Slavic Croatian heritage. They wanted to stop him from following in his father's footsteps. More than anything else I would like to believe that Mihovil is alive," I said fetching a sigh.

"We have to solve the riddle of his disappearance," Khalil said confidently.

"I'll look for Dr. Sandalic," I said gazing at Khalil.

"In the morning we are going on the first ferry-boat to Zadar in order to arrive before the beginning of the faculty lectures," Khalil responded, confirming my thoughts that Dr. Sandalic was our last hope in the search for Mihovil.

WE WENT TO THE Faculty of Philosophy early in the morning. We found Dr. Sandalic in his office before he held his exams. He was sitting at the table creating the student schedule. I knocked on the door greeting Dr. Sandalic. The professor looked me up and down and said calmly, "I was expecting you, Dr. Antonija."

He took off his glasses and then approached Khalil. He hugged him warmly and continued, "I am glad that our friend is with you."

"It seems like forever since the last time I saw you," Khalil greeted him with friendship.

I was watching Dr. Sandalic and Khalil while they were exchanging their first words. I realized that something bigger than friendship bound them together and that Dr. Sandalic as well was a part of the group of Khalil's *celestial police*.

"What news do you bring me?" Dr. Sandalic turned to us, unable to restrain curiosity.

"Not very good," I said with a sad expression on my face.

"Matija, how did Mihovil end up?" Khalil said impatiently.

Dr. Sandalic sighed deeply and continued, "The secret police killed Mihovil. His father's fate caught up with him."

Hearing these words, I sobbed silently. I still cherished the hope that the body found on the Kornati Islands might not have been Mihovil's. I interrupted Dr. Sandalic. I turned to him raising my voice, "That cannot be true. Didn't they kill Ishmael?"

Dr. Sandalic came closer and gently caressed my hair.

"Antonija, the *DNA* tests confirmed that the body found on the Kornati Islands was the body of Mihovil. I am truly sorry. You have to be strong."

I exerted all my strength to restrain myself from crying. I let Dr. Sandalic continue, "Your Mihovil actually died at the moment his double took all his powers."

I looked at Dr. Sandalic. I continued barely uttering a word, "So you knew everything? Please tell us what you found out."

Dr. Sandalic coughed and continued persuasively, "On that morning when Mihovil disappeared, I arrived at the library a little bit early. I wanted to check if grandmother Lucija's book was in its place. The door was slightly opened. Mihovil was inside. He had a strange expression on his face. When I approached him he was sitting with his head buried in a book.

He looked up at me with his piercing cold eyes. His gaze almost rendered me unconscious. It was obvious that he had acquired supernatural powers. I tried to snatch the book from him, but accidentally tore a page from the book."

The page with the ritual mantras? I said to myself. "Why didn't you tell us?" I yelled in despair.

"I didn't want to tell anyone until I straightened everything out. I was afraid that Mihovil or the one who took him over could misuse his powers."

"What did you do with the page?" I asked Dr. Sandalic.

"I put it in an envelope and left it in the desk drawer in this room. Mihovil's first name and surname were on the envelope. Unfortunately the envelope suddenly disappeared. I noticed it was missing at the beginning of the last summer."

"I beg your pardon! What does it all mean?" I turned to Dr. Sandalic and said suspiciously.

"Arriving one day to work, I found the desk drawer open. Everything was jumbled up in the drawer. The envelope with the page was missing. I am sure the secret police did it."

"Are you sure?" I looked at him questioningly.

"Antonija, I know how they operate. Don't worry about them. I'll deal with them myself. We have some unsettled, old scores. My family underwent a similar fate as that which befell Mihovil's family. They killed my father who was a well-respected historian. He dealt with national issues in historical science opposing the mainstream, scientific thought of the time. Although the official report says that he drowned, I know he actually was killed by the secret police."

"I am truly sorry," I responded giving Dr. Sandalic a pensive look. "Don't you think that someone among their agents might have read the ritual words and misused their powers?"

"There is no fear of that. They couldn't have misused them. The ritual mantras can only have an effect on the chosen ones."

"Could you explain?"

"People like you and your Mihovil can catch the rhythm of the mantras since you vibrate at higher frequencies."

"Yes, I understand. Mihovil said that I was the last speaker of an archaic dialect of a primordial language that was preserved in the linguistic tradition of the ancient Liburnians. When chanted, it sounds like the meditation mantra chanting that revives the rhythm of the ancient Vedas."

"For that reason you are valuable to us. We shouldn't lose you."

"No, no, I won't give up! I am of the blood of the holy race, the ancient Liburnians!" I said with confidence and then continued, "Tell us finally what happened to Mihovil?"

"After I tore the page, Mihovil suddenly became invisible. He just disappeared. Then I called Khalil. You know what happened next."

"But I saw him in New York! His warmth was all around me!"

"It was Mihovil's ethereal body, and the other one was his shadow."

"Ishmael? Does it mean that Ishmael is alive?" I exclaimed with excitement.

"Yes, and you are the only one who can stop him. Go back to your Mihovil. Free him from his shadow and become united with him," Dr. Sandalic said.

"We need your help, Antonija. If you can liberate Mihovil, the *shadow of evil* will never overwhelm him again. He was under the influence of the evil beings. If you manage to pull him out of their embrace, you will save not only him but all humanity from their sinister intentions," Khalil said after a long pause.

"And save your people," Dr. Sandalic added.

"How?" I looked at him questioningly.

"Mihovil is waiting for you. He is waiting for you at the place from where the androgynous beings similar to you come from. Only you two together can function as a whole. Liberating Mihovil from his shadow, you two will become one and will take away the evil beings' potential powers," Dr Sandalic said firmly.

Hearing these words, I listened to the whisper of my heart. I felt the gentle call of the light of truth: I understood that by awakening myself and unfolding the God within, I will win the battle for the human soul on Earth.

MEMORIES BEGAN TO FLOOD my mind. I saw Mihovil illuminated by a candle flame. While he was moving the candle over the back of the page with the ritual mantras of the book of grandmother Lucija, I was slowly leaving the body. I saw a dark shadow envelop Mihovil. I heard myself utter the ritual words Naga Shakti for the last time. That took me for a moment into the Kingdom of Naga Spirits. I knew that the only way to rescue Mihovil from evil was for me to return there.

Khalil interrupted my train of thought.

"Antonija, you are going to succeed. Your ancestors are by your side. You have to do this for your sake and the sake of your people!"

"I am sure you will! You will remove the stigma

from your people and save the face of the ancient Liburnians!" Dr. Sandalic said solemnly.

I looked at Dr. Sandalic. His eyes mirrored the sparkle of silence. Illuminated by the glow of the tiny sparkles that were emitting from other souls, I felt connected with them in the Eye of the Universe. I took a long breath.

Before starting to chant the mantra and leave this world to go toward Mihovil, I turned to Dr. Sandalic for the last time and said, "I'll free Mihovil from his shadow and I'll overpower Him. It will be my last battle."

IN MIHOVIL'S EMBRACE

I fell into sleep. I found myself in my hometown, Preko. I was lying down on the rock, sea cliff, intoxicated by the scent of salt and the beauty of an azure blue sea. The immortal glory of my ancestors revived in my mind. I brought back memories of a celestial being with golden bracelets on each of his four arms, around his wrist, and another one on his upper arm. He was sitting in a lotus pose and mumbling. I sat at his feet. I grabbed a string of red beads and started repeating the prayer after Him. After each uttered syllable, one bead after another began to fall apart. The more I chanted the mantra, the beads became more like drops of blood falling onto my wet feet. Then the blue sky turned into a dark sky. High waves came up. A gust of wind caused the door to the abyss to open. I was violently thrown off far away into the space of the Universe. I could have only imagined the Earth as a tiny dot in the shadow of a bright light ray. A blinking light connected me by invisible forces to Mother Earth. In the rhythm of my inhalations and exhalations, all my fear, anguish, grief and hope were carried toward this tiny, Earth dot. Under the luminous umbrella of light, I was protected from the deadly void in the surrounding space. A flickering and sparkling light shone forth from the Earth's innocuous face. Then I saw with my inner eye the ring of condensed ether particles that appeared around the Earth like a halo on its outer edges. Stunned, I was overcome by the glittering force that was welling up out of the radiating ring formation. An unreal figure was glimmering through it. Awakened for a moment in divine silence, I discerned the face of Ishmael: I was looking through two menacing black eyes, catching a beam of light pouring with its golden threads from the dark immensity. Behind his motionless face the contours of a pale-faced being began to appear. I could feel inhumane coldness coming off him. I approached him, but he didn't move. I called him, but he stared at me speechless. He quivered only after he heard my voice. I felt the Divine Presence. The voice was vibrating, re-echoing the tones of the etheric music of the spheres, "He cannot harm you. You will defeat him by the energy of love. In all the Universe there is no more powerful spark than the spark of love enkindled in the heart of the pure soul."

The voice silenced. The air still seemed to be full of

the Divine Presence, a seductive fullness He revealed. The harmonious sound of silence was coming from the background. Listening to the sound of pure existence, I went back to the Source. In the moment of Divine grace, catching the gleam of a purple light, kindled in me the sparkle of His love. I was imbued with bliss. I was radiating it. The evil being that was behind the Ishmael face suddenly started disintegrating. I felt the rush of energy welling out of my arms. It was like a stream of light made up of all the colors of the spectrum. It was spreading out further and further. I realized that there was no end to it, that I was the light itself. I felt connected to the other beings of light. I saw the faces of Khalil, Ibrahim, David, Dr. Sandalic, the faces of my dearest *celestial police* companions looking at me. They all were giving me strength. I knew I was in the center of the Naga Kingdom because I was at the doorstep of the hall of pure gold. As soon as I stepped into it, thousands of lights began to shine. They represented different deities. They were led by the serpentine protectress of the submarine world. I stopped in front of her, bowing low before her. Her pearly eyes glared sending me thoughts, "Your love is waiting for you. If you go towards him, you will unite yourself with your Divine Fiancé and realize your true Self, but you will forever stay in the world of your ascended brothers. Together with them, you will continue working for the well-being of the people of Earth until all the people unite their consciousness and the whole Earth frees itself from the dark forces."

The Queen of the submarine world finished. A figure came out of the eastern door. I didn't hesitate to rush into his arms. He was approaching slowly as his shape became more defined. He appeared complete for a moment. It seemed as if it lasted forever. He wrapped his arms around my waist. He let my hair down and put a crown of pure pearls on my head. As he was kissing my face and invoking the song of the ancestors, he uttered in silence, "You will be mine forever."

Mihovil was gazing at me with his deep, opal, black crystal, clear eye. A hymn reverberated. The brighter and brighter light was spreading from all directions when in a twinkling the contours of my Liburnian Goddesses appeared. Their fluttering scent enveloped us, a gentle mist enfolded us, and we were drawn into their circle. Imbued with vibrations of eternal love, we began our love dance. We dove into the whirlpool of timeless passion carried by the Spiral energy of God's Love. We were falling unto unreached depths of consciousness, rising to the surface of our hearts, united in a beam of light. We would disappear with the silent cry of spiritual longing, revealed in the fullness hidden in the eternal murmur of our souls. United in beauty that was beaming from the horizon of eternity, we were sending to Earth and the whole Universe the energy of love. Its rhythm was reverberating in the song of Pandit Sati who was chanting silently, softly, with a ring of a far-away place. When the last sounds of the celestial symphony became quiet, leaving behind only the scent of blessed silence, the doors of the golden bars closed and after them the passage to the endless Kingdom of Naga Spirits.

EPILOGUE

Many years had passed since my ascension into the Kingdom of Spirits. It was the year 2026 on Earth. An elderly man was sitting on the shores of the Mediterranean south of Beirut watching the advancing waves from the open ocean that were hitting the boiling beach sand. Wandering around, he ran his gaze down the sparkling foam in a gentle caress. He caught glimpses of movement on the waves. He stood up and approached the sea. Standing motionless, he was listening to the shattering waves. As the waves were breaking on the shore, he approached closer to the sea. Suddenly he saw in front of him an exceedingly beautiful, serpentine sea siren. It was the moment he was yearning for. The siren looked at him and before riding back on the top of a wave, she left a trail of sea foam. She sent a message with her tail, "Khalil, we won. The *shadow of evil* will never again hang over the Earth." He swam after the siren. He knew he could give her his soul since the time of eternity had come.

AFTERWORD

Andreja Austin:
The Last Woman Warrior of the Liburnians
MYSTICAL NOVEL

From Ugljan via war-torn Beirut to the United Nations in New York – all for the sake of love which could only overcome evil, in all dimensions . . .

Behind the love at first glance between Antonija and Mihovil, there is a secret about their common ancestral origin from a small nation of the Liburnians. The Liburnians ruled over the Adriatic Sea between the 9th and 5th centuries B.C. Antonija found a clue of a previous high culture in a book belonging to her grandmother in which she connected to higher vibrational beings. They watched over her as ancestral spirits. When Mihovil mysteriously disappeared, Antonija, a medical doctor, searched after him and joined the Mission for the Refugees in war-torn Beirut. Following in his footsteps, she came to Jerusalem and the United Nations in New York. After discovering that Mihovil was overpowered by the unearthly, evil forces that threatened to take over the Earth, Antonija found out how she could stop them with her love.

This is a novel about love, carried by the wings of pure light and the moments of ecstasy at the threshold of an endless dimension. It is also a novel of the suffering of the children in Beirut, the agents of hidden identity and a unique resolution. This all takes place at the same time in the centers of power in New York and on the small island of Croatia. *The Last Woman Warrior of the Liburnians* is a novel whose genre cannot easily be defined. Acquainting us with distant lands and dedicated people, Andreja Austin demonstrates profound imagination, combining elements of mystical, crime and love novels. She intertwines her story with knowledge of mythology, astrology and history, setting the plot on several levels – in the real world of conflicts, war and murder, and in the spheres of higher frequency beings where the mythological beings live.

The novel, *The Last Woman Warrior of the Liburnians*, uses reality and imagination to tell an adventure with dangerous situations and intense emotions, as well as with communication with Gods and the world beyond. Andreja Austin revives in her novel an archetypal woman character who is ready to go to the ends of the Earth and beyond because of her love, to immerse herself in timeless passion, while embraced by a loved one and carried by the Spiral energy of God's Love.

Sandra Pocrnic-Mlakar

ABOUT THE AUTHOR

ANDREJA AUSTIN IS A CROATIAN AMERICAN living in Santa Fe, New Mexico. She holds a PhD degree in Russian Literature. She also translates and publishes popular spiritual literature in Croatia. The author's first novel, *The Last Woman Warrior of the Liburnians*, was first published in Croatia in 2017.

Printed in the USA
CPSIA information can be obtained
at www.ICGtesting.com
CBHW030856150624
9994CB00004B/23